Two-Point Conversion

Rangers Football
Book 4

Kameron Claire

Snuggle Whore Press, LLC

To all the Witty, Wicked & Wild Readers...
Never let them silence our Witty tongues,
Never let them shame our Wicked needs,
Never let them stop our Wild deeds.

Thank you for the love and support!

ROCKY MOUNTAIN
RANGERS

Prologue

"I say we invite that one, and that one and, of course, the redhead over there back to our hotel."

Rex shakes his head. "Coach will have our ass if he finds out we brought a bunch of strippers home with us."

"Dancers—" Jepson flashes a brunette his Sunday school smile "—and the coach isn't invited."

"Dancers, whatever." Rex rolls his eyes.

"Which one do you like, Jaxson?"

Jaxson shrugs and takes a draw off his beer. "I don't care."

"Sure you do. You want the redhead, don't you?" Jepson taunts. "He always goes for the redhead."

Jaxson rolls his eyes. "Actually, I was digging the blonde."

"I already call dibs on the blonde." Jepson smirks, his eye contact hard across the table at his brother.

"Of course you did," Jaxson mutters.

The blonde in question comes up and flashes the table a big smile. "Anyone looking for a lap dance?"

"Actually, honey, we were hoping for something a bit more intimate." Jepson leans forward.

She tsks and throws him a placating smile. "I'm sure you are, but this is not that kind of establishment."

"I'm sure for the right price it could be any kind of establishment we want."

"Where are you boys from?"

"Spring City, Colorado. What about you?"

"I'm Nashville, born and raised, sugar."

Jepson lets his eyes trail down her body. "What time do you get off work?"

"Why?" She straightens, putting more distance between her and him.

"The boys would love to see Music Row. Since you're homegrown, you could show us the places only the locals go."

"Every place on Music Row is good, and they are easy to find. Just walk a straight line and follow your nose or your ears, depending upon what you're looking for."

"But don't you want to entertain a couple of big, badass football players?"

Plastering on a sweet smile, she bats her eyelashes. "My boyfriend is a big, badass football player."

"From Nashville?" Rex arches his brow.

"You damn right," she replies.

"Yeah, but Nashville sucks," Jepson chuckles. "We're going to be national champions, honey. Wouldn't you like to suck the dick of a winner at least once this year?"

Her smile fades, and she turns to walk away. Jepson reaches out and grabs her hand—the one thing you're not allowed to do.

"Man, don't touch the dancers," Rylie says, putting his drink down. He looks over his shoulder at security, which is walking their way. "We're not in Denver and the women here don't know you like that, so keep your hands to yourself."

"Fuck you, choirboy," Jepson releases her hand and puts his hands in his lap. "Sorry honey. I just want to apologize. I didn't mean to infer you'll be sucking my dick. It could be one of my teammates."

She looks over our heads and shakes her head, letting the security guard know it's okay for the moment. "You're an asshole."

Jepson smiles. "Yeah, but I'm a hot asshole."

She rolls her eyes and walks away at about the same time a waitress walks up with another round of drinks. They are not supposed to be drinking tonight, and yet Jepson's on his third whiskey on the rocks. His twin brother Jaxson is nursing his one and only beer and Devlin, Rylie, and Rex are drinking Diet Coke.

"We should get out of here and check out a couple of local artists on our walk back to the hotel," Devlin says, throwing down a twenty and standing, brokering no questions that he's leaving. Rylie also stands, throwing down his own Jaxson, following Devlin out.

Rex rubs the back of his neck. "What do you guys think?"

Prologue Continued
Jaxson

My brother scoffs. "Let the choirboys go home. You know, the rumor is that Rylie used to be wild before he put Deacon Scott in the hospital."

I shrug. "He's got a kid and responsibilities now."

Jepson sighs, his eyes going back to the blonde who is within earshot. "I wonder if she'd let me put a baby in her?"

"Yeah, that's all we need in this world—more *yous* running around."

"Come on, man. Let's get out of here." Rex tosses what's left of the napkin he's been tearing up on the table. "We have a better chance of getting laid by some random chick on Broadway than we do here."

I stay in my seat and say nothing as I watch my brother. He's in a mood tonight and god knows why this time. I never know what's going to set him off. Never know what puts him in a bad mood. All I know is that when he's like this, I have to stay close or else who knows what kind of trouble he's going to start.

I am my brother's keeper.

I would get the phrase tattooed across my shoulder blades, except that would definitely start a fight between us.

Jepson frowns at the blonde who is actively ignoring him, downs the last of his drink, and throws fifty dollars down on the table. "Fuck it. Let's get out of here."

I send up a silent prayer of thanks, hoping we get out of here without another incident. If I can get him back to his room, I can contain any fallout from the meltdown he's on the verge of having. He needs to be medicated, not that I'll ever be able to tell him that.

He would never hear it from me.

We walk out together—me bringing up the rear as usual—but we don't get more than ten feet out the door when a guy a few inches taller and at least forty pounds heavier approaches us with way too much aggression to be a coincidence. "Are you the asshole hitting on my Darla?"

"Which one is Darla?" Jepson says with a teasing tilt to his lips.

The big guy's eyes narrow. "I heard you were talking shit about the Nashville Notes."

"Yeah, because they suck."

"We'll see what happens on the field tomorrow."

It's at this moment I recognize this behemoth of a man. This is Rick Steward—defensive lineman for the

Nashville Notes—and I'm guessing the blonde is his girlfriend.

Perfect.

"We were just leaving," I say, causing the big guy's eyes to slide from Jepson to me.

"I've heard about you two. The Masters twins. Word is, the ugly one is a decent guy and the pretty boy is an asshole. Seems like the rumors are true."

Jepson steps forward. "What the fuck did you say about my brother?"

I sigh, because of course he would use me as a reason to start a fight. Wrapping my hand around his bicep, I try to pull him back and give Rex a fucking *help me* look.

Rex steps between them. "Not tonight, man. We get into a fight and we're all fucked. Let's save it for the field tomorrow, huh?"

Rick smiles as a bouncer steps up to our group. He tilts his head toward the back of the parking lot. "Take it off the property, Rick."

"Fuck it, let's go," Jepson walks in the direction the bouncer points to before I have a chance to stop him.

"Shit," I hiss and chase after him. We only take a couple of steps before big hands are on my back, pushing me into Jepson. We both stumble forward, bouncing off the concrete wall near the side door.

I turn in time to catch a right hook across my left cheek and eye.

At the same time, a high-pitched squeal comes from behind us—a flurry of blonde hair and shiny silver material climbing onto Jepson's back, screaming obscenities.

It's over before it truly starts. Two bouncers pull the blonde dancer—Darla—off Jepson's back, at the same time backing Rick up after he sucker punches me.

"Get off the property," the second bouncer, the one not instigating the fight, says to Rex, who pulls both of us away to shove us into a waiting taxi.

The entire altercation takes less than two minutes and yet my cheek throbs and I'm positive I'm going to end up with a black eye.

Just another day in the life as Jepson Masters' twin brother.

Fuck my life.

Chapter One
Jaxson

"Masters, times two," Darius pokes his head around the lockers and into our line of sight. "Coach's office. Now."

Sighing, I set my shower kit into my locker and slide my shorts up my legs. Three lockers down, my brother is naked and looking at me with a raised eyebrow.

Dammit. I knew it.

I shake my head and slip on my shower shoes. He wraps a towel around his waist and slips on his sandals, following me down the hallway.

Coach Monroe looks up from his computer screen. The look on his face tells me he is not pleased. "I just got off the phone with Coach Whitman from the Nashville Notes, and apparently you two were involved in an altercation Saturday night."

My brother shakes his head. "I wouldn't call it an altercation."

"Really? So how do you explain Jaxson's black eye and the scratches on your back?"

"A fun night with a spirited young lady?" Jepson grins, thinking his charming smile and juvenile humor are going to get us out of trouble with our boss.

I know better.

"Shut the fuck up, Jepson!" Coach slams his fist down on his desk. "You have a lot of potential, but I will not allow your bullshit to bring this organization down. Not this season. You don't want to take this job seriously? Maybe we need to find you a new home."

Jepson's smile falls. "Sorry, Coach."

Coach Monroe shakes his head. "The head office is sick of your shit. No more fuck-ups. No more bad publicity or headline fodder for the tabloids. If you want to make a home with the Rocky Mountain Rangers, your entire lives need to be football and only fucking football from now on. Do you understand?"

"Yes, Coach," we say at the same time.

"If we have to have this conversation again, it won't be you and I talking. The next conversation will be with Deacon Scott."

Well, shit. That's the threat of all threats and a one-way ticket to the unemployment line.

He picks up a business card and hands it to me. "The President of Communications made you an appointment for next Monday, one pm. The team wants the two of you to co-sponsor a local charity as part of your public relations commitment. All the guys are doing it, but Ms. Scott thinks if you keep your noses clean, they could spin the whole twin brother thing into a positive public image for you and the team. No other team in the league has brothers playing on the same team, much less twins. Use this opportunity to your advantage."

Jepson and I glance at the name and number on the card.

Maryanne Merryweather.

This has to be a joke.

Coach Monroe sighs. "Hit the showers, Jepson. Jaxson, stand by."

I watch as my brother leaves the office. Right before he closes the door, our eyes connect, his unspoken words clear. *You better have my back.*

I know the look well. I've gotten it hundreds of times over the years.

I stand by stoically, my hands clasped in front of my hips.

Coach leans back in his chair and stares at me. "Your coaches tell me it's time to bring you up as a first-string cornerback. Your performance is phenomenal on game days and our defensive line could use your talents, but we also feel you are holding back during practice to stay under the radar."

My heart races in my chest. This is a dream and a nightmare unfolding before me.

The coach continues. "While you and Jepson are talented players, you have an actual future in football, Jaxson. Don't let some fucked up sense of loyalty ruin it for you. Jepson's bullshit is not only going to get you in trouble with this organization, but he's going to tarnish your reputation within the league. I understand he's your brother and I understand he's your twin—which supposedly makes you guys closer than brothers—but he is not good for you."

Coach Monroe rubs his neck and rolls his shoulders. "Part of the reason we picked you both up, outside of your talents, was the gimmick. There are plenty of brothers playing on different teams in the league, but to have identical twins playing opposing positions on the same team, covering special teams in both directions, was a great marketing ploy. Unfortunately, it hasn't worked out that way because the only headline fodder tied to the Masters twins is chaos. You need to make some decisions about what it is you want for your future regardless of Jepson. I suggest you take the next few weeks to think about what your position within this organization looks like."

"Yes, Coach." My mind whirls with the crossroad I'm standing on. Either be the best I can be on the field, move up the ranks, piss off my brother and destroy an already tenuous relationship with him, or hold back and watch my professional football career disintegrate.

"Go on. Get out of my office," Coach dismisses me without so much as a second glance.

I walk out of his office and down the hallway to find Jepson waiting outside the locker room door, a towel still wrapped around his waist. While my body is tattooed and scarred, his is pristine—the clean original copy of what I should look like. We both have light blond hair and bright blue eyes, but his face is unblemished and his nose is straight. I have twice broken my nose, and I have a scar running from my left ear to the corner of my mouth, as well as several under my eye and along my neck—most of which I got in the accident.

"What did he say?" Jepson pushes off the wall as I approach.

I shrug. "The organization is sick of our shit."

"Yeah, I was there for that part. What did he say after I left?"

Walking past him, I stop when he grabs my bicep. "He said I need to be thinking about my future with the organization."

"Shit, man," Jepson lets go, assuming the worst. "I'm sorry."

"Yeah." I enter the mostly empty locker room and plop down on the bench in front of my gear.

Jepson sits beside me, keeping his voice low. "Seriously, Jaxs, I'm sorry. I know this is my fault. My temper, my arrogance, and my bullshit get us into these *altercations* every time. I'll do better. I promise."

All things I've heard before.

He smacks my shoulder and stands up. "Come on. Let's shower, grab a burger with Rex and then play Xbox for a couple of hours. Tomorrow we'll bring the heat and show the Rangers they want us as part of their organization."

Again, all things I've heard before, but I'm desperate to believe him. I reluctantly nod and grab my shower kit. "Okay."

"Jepson," I call from the bottom of the stairs. "We've got to go. We're going to be late."

My brother comes out of his room wearing slacks with a button-down in his hand. "Can't, man. Cover for me."

"What the fuck do you mean, cover for you? This is a mandatory appointment. We have to do this."

Jepson slides on his shirt and bounces down the stairs, a tad too peppy to not mean trouble. "Man, I do not want to spend two hours with some cardigan-wearing sixty-year-old cat lady named Maryanne Merryweather looking over sad photos of bedridden kids or kenneled dogs. I promise—you pick the charity and I will be at every event with a smile on my face. But..." He pulls his phone out of his slacks and brings up his text messaging app, flashing me a picture of a beautiful brunette in a fluffy pink towel. "Crystal invited me over for a little afternoon delight."

"Isn't she married?" I recognize her from a dance club we frequent downtown. She's one of their bartenders and a woman Jepson has been desperate to fuck for months.

"She was, but now she's separated and in need of some stress relief." He waggles his eyebrows.

"Dammit, Jepson. If Coach finds out you ditched this meeting, there's going to be hell to pay."

"He won't, and if he does, I'll come up with a brilliant

excuse that has nothing to do with you." Jepson slides his phone back into his pocket and clasps his hands together. "Please, Jaxs. You know how badly I've been lusting after this woman. Please cover for me. I promise I'll be at every other meeting. I'll clean up dog shit if that's what the charity requires—" he pauses "—on second thought, please don't pick a charity that requires cleaning up dog shit."

I sigh. "Fine. We don't pick the charity today, anyway. We're just going over all the choices and filling out a questionnaire about our passions, which I'm guessing for you will be single moms of the pole dancing variety."

He snorts. "I also have a passion for pusssssssssy cats."

"Your dick is going to get us in a lot of trouble one day."

"Thank god I always wrap him up." Jepson runs back up the stairs, leaving me to shake my head.

Twenty-five minutes later, I'm walking into an office in the middle of a twenty-year-old strip mall. There's a taco shop on one side and an empty tax prep office on the other. The inside is chaos—tables riddled with papers, pens, binders and poster boards giving me a high school science fair vibe. "Hello?"

Out of a back office pops a stacked vision in pink pastel, her dark auburn hair piled high on her head. She's wearing a tank top that's stretched beyond capacity over her full breasts and she has the plumpest, kissable heart-shaped lips I've ever seen in my life. "Oh, you're early. Hold on one second."

She darts back into her office, coming out a minute later wearing a pink and black argyle sweater buttoned up over her plentiful cleavage. "I'm sorry it's so hot in here. The A/C took a nap this morning and the HVAC guy won't be here until later this afternoon."

Is it warm in here? I thought it was my reaction to her. "No worries."

"Let's sit at the table in the back where the fan is to stay comfortable," She motions to a table, walking in front of me to give me a glimpse of her curvy body and mesmerizing backside that swings in a hypnotic rhythm with every step she takes. I'm nowhere near the horn dog my brother is, but I am a red-blooded male and everything about this woman has me taking notice.

"Are you Maryanne Merryweather?"

"That's me." She turns and smiles, offering me her dainty hand. "I'm sorry, normally I take time to research my clients before our first meeting, but Deidre dropped this in my lap and I was busy with other customers. Are you Jepson or Jaxson Masters?"

"Jaxson." I shake her hand, her grip a lot firmer than I would have thought, although her hand is soft.

"Where's your brother?" She motions to a seat and I begrudgingly drop her hand to sit across from her.

"He's not going to make it today, but sends his apologies."

"Oh, well, should we reschedule?"

"No. I can do this without him." I look into her brown eyes framed by thick dark lashes, a hint of color dotting her cheeks as she smiles back at me. She's got an innocent girl-next-door charm about her freshly scrubbed face, her sweet smile disarmingly seductive. Then I notice a drop of sweat running down her neck, over her collarbone, underneath her sweater and between her cleavage. At the same time, a drop slides down between my shoulder blades. I normally run hot, so I don't notice when I sweat and yet something deep within me wants to capture the runaway moisture dampening her skin with my tongue. Preferably as it heads farther south. "If you're hot, you can take off your sweater."

Her blush deepens. "If I had known the A/C was going to conk out today, I would have worn a different top. I don't normally wear tank tops with clients. It's not very professional."

"You don't have to be formal with me. I rarely dress to impress." I smile, trying to conjure up one of Jepson's Sunday school grins.

Sucking her plump bottom lip between her teeth, she glances around. "Let me grab a couple of ice waters."

She comes back to the table with the top three buttons of her sweater undone and offers me a cool bottle of flavored water. "Should we get started?"

"Sure."

"Why does the organization want you to co-sponsor a charity? Is it rare for two brothers to be on the same team?"

"Yes, but it is even rarer for those brothers to be identical twins."

Her mouth drops open. "There are two of you?"

I chuckle. "You really don't know anything about us, do you?"

"I really don't. Again, I apologize. The last month has been crazy for me. Helping football players sign on to existing charities or set up their own is a bigger job than I was expecting." She grabs a wad of papers and fans herself with them.

"This is new for you?"

"Yes. I started three weeks ago, hence the temporary space," she waves her paper fan to the lacking office space. "I mean, I've been managing charitable organizations for years, but not for the Rangers."

"Where do we begin?" I lean back in the chair, realizing she has the fan centered on me, which is why I'm not sweltering like her. With only my welfare in mind, she's making herself uncomfortable. Wow. I'm not used to someone deferring to my needs. Not with a brother who always has to be first, always has to win.

I stand up and pull the plunger, allowing the fan to oscillate as needed. The papers on the desk flutter, but I move a stapler to weigh them down.

She sighs. "Thank you. I was so tempted to take off my sweater."

Well, fuck me and good deeds.

"As I said, you don't have to be formal with me."

Smiling, she undoes the rest of her buttons, hands me a form on a clipboard, and then opens up her laptop. "Usually I start with an interview, so I can recommend the best charities for you. We can either team up with an existing one and offer you and your brother up as ambassadors of sorts to the charity—kind of like many football players do with the United Way. Or, we can set up something specific that is meaningful to you and your brother. For instance, if you have a family member with a chronic illness or disability that has affected your family's lives. Having a personal connection helps drum up support and tells a great, heartwarming story. I suppose you can answer eighty percent of the questions for your brother."

I look over the form on the clipboard with a dozen questions on it. My brother doesn't like to share personal details from our childhood, which means unless I want a fight, I also don't share. While keeping my feelings bottled up only makes me more of an introvert than I already am, not expressing himself is what makes Jepson volatile.

I one hundred percent believe that is the reason he blows up from time to time.

"How about we jot down the basics today and go from there?" My eyes come up from the page to lock with hers, her gaze tracing over my features, probably taking in all my scars. I'm used to being stared at with a critical eye, but the way she looks at me is thoughtful and nurturing— as if she wants to crawl into my lap and hug me.

She flashes me another sweet smile and a war of emotions runs rampant through my body. Blood rushes south as my mind conjures up images of snuggling with her on the couch, her plush body nestled on my thighs, her ass cradling my hardening cock. I could kiss her for hours, nibbling on her plump lips as my hands explore her lush curves.

"Mr. Masters?" Maryanne pulls me from my daydream.

I shake my head and discreetly lay the clipboard in my lap. "What?"

"Where did you grow up?" Her fingers are on the keyboard.

"Oh. Uh, a small town outside of Columbia, South Carolina." I look down at the list of questions again, knowing I can't answer a couple of them. I'm unwilling to lie, but that doesn't mean I can spew the truth without repercussions.

"Any other siblings?" she continues, oblivious to my dirty thoughts.

"No."

"What about your parents?"

"What about them?" I pseudo-snap.

She frowns. "Are you close?"

"Not particularly," I say in a softer tone, but my words are no less harsh.

Maryanne looks down at her hands and nods. "I understand."

"No, you don't," I shake my head. "I'm sorry, but my brother is a private person and I know using details about our family as part of a charity will piss him off."

"I have no intention of airing your family details as part of your charity. The questions are supposed to be icebreakers, so I can get to know you, that's all."

"Are you saying this is off the record?"

She purposefully makes a show of bringing her hands off her keyboard and closing the laptop lid. Turning in her chair, she faces the fan head-on, which blows the sides of her sweater back from her chest. "Maybe we should just talk and get to know each other?"

I smile. "I'd like that, but first, have you eaten lunch yet?"

"No. Why? Did you hear my tummy rumble?" She blushes.

Chuckling, I place the clipboard on her desk. My cock softened to the point of decency. "No, but mine's about to. Is the taco shop next door any good?"

"Actually, yeah."

"Can I buy you a couple of tacos?"

Her face lights up. "Only if they have A/C."

"Deal."

Chapter Two
Maryanne

One perk of my new job with the Rangers is I get to sit and talk with handsome, well-built men of all ages and sizes. Unfortunately, most of them are too young for me, like the hottie sitting across from me right now. He's got to be six or seven years my junior, if not more.

I'll be thirty-three next month and I'm guessing he's twenty-five, maybe.

That doesn't mean I can't appreciate the goods.

Jaxson Masters is a fine specimen of a man. Tall, well-built, with beautiful blue eyes and the sweetest dimples in an otherwise ruggedly handsome face. He has a few old scars that I'm sure come with a serious story to them. They are too big and deep to be from falling off his bike as a kid.

He also has tattoos, judging by the ink peeking out of his collar. Between the scars and the ink, he could have a hard, menacing veneer to him, but his beautiful eyes and dazzling smile are too sweet to see anything other than a slightly introverted gentleman in front of me.

I can't believe there are two of them.

We're settled in a U-shaped booth with a few feet of space between us—a basket of chips and two sides of salsa on the table. He's drinking water while I have calorie-heavy sweet horchata. Embarrassingly, I ordered a fried chimichanga before he ordered a healthy chicken and shrimp taco salad.

"I guess you have to be careful about what you eat as a football player, huh?"

He shrugs. "I have pancreatitis, so I try to watch my fatty red meat and alcohol intake to avoid flare-ups and gallstones."

"Oh, wow. Is that hereditary?" I ask as I scoop a chip full of salsa, praying I don't dribble on my chest as I lift it to my mouth. That would one hundred percent be a thing I would do, especially in front of a fitness and health-conscious man like Jaxson.

"No, it's just me."

"How old were you when you were diagnosed?"

Jaxson stares down at the table. "Fourteen."

I'm a licensed therapist—I mean, I was, but I am no longer since I let my licensure lapse once I stopped actively practicing, choosing to get involved in establishing and auditing charitable organizations over owning and operating my own office. I love talking to people and helping them work through their stuff. But I found myself a bit too empathetic about some of my clients, taking their problems home with me night after night.

Sometimes, I was more affected by their personal turmoil than they were. It was only after my friend told me I was rehashing other people's problems—none of my own—that I knew it wasn't the career for me.

However, I still have the training and an eye for certain behavioral traits, and this is something that causes Jaxson pain. "Fourteen? That's so young for such a heavy, life-altering change."

He brings his eyes up to meet mine. "Monitoring my diet is the least of my problems."

I give him a patient smile and reach for his hand, sliding my fingers over his to give him a friendly squeeze. "Do you want to talk about it?"

To my surprise, he grasps my hand, holding it almost lovingly, if not a bit desperately. "I've never talked about it before."

"Anything you say to me stays between us." I don't pull my hand away and although it's all kinds of wrong, I rather enjoy his touch.

He chews on his lip, staring down at our intertwined fingers. "I was at school our freshman year and started throwing up in class. Jepson ran me to the bathroom and called our mother. When she came to get me, he wanted to come home with us, but she forced him to go back to class. On the drive home, I puked up blood—literally spewing it all over the dashboard. My mom panicked, lost control, and drove us over the medium into oncoming traffic. An eighteen-wheeler hit the back end of our truck, spinning and flipping us into a ditch. I only remember bits and pieces after that. They rushed us to the hospital, my dad and Jepson arriving sometime later. I had lost a lot of blood and they used Jepson as my personal blood bank, tethered to me and a machine instead of in the room with our mother as she died."

The muscles in his jaw flex, a lone tear falling down his cheek. I say nothing, using my thumb to rub softly over the back of his hand.

"I've never said all of that out loud before." He brings his head up, his eyes coming to mine. "How did you—"

Our server walks up with our orders, dropping a hot plate in front of me. "Is there anything else I can get you?"

I shake my head and wait until they walk away. "Why haven't you talked about this before?"

He shrugs. "Our father is not much of a talker and anytime I brought it up, Jepson got angry. I think he blames me for her death."

"I'm sure that's not true." I know better than to say that as a therapist, but the words roll off my tongue all the same.

Jaxson sighs, bringing our joined hands up to his mouth. He kisses my fingers and then lets go, his demeanor changing before my eyes. "Let's eat, huh?"

I know when to let something go and when to dig in my heels, and at this moment, Jaxson needs me to let this go.

"Okay," Leaning forward, I kiss his scarred cheek before turning to my lunch.

I have a forkful of chimichanga up to my lips when I realize he's staring at me. "What?"

"Why'd you do that?"

"Why'd I do what?"

"Kiss me."

"Oh—" A hot blush hits my cheeks. "I'm so sorry. I didn't even think about it. That was super unprofessional."

He grins. "So, you're saying you couldn't help yourself?"

He's teasing me and I like it. "No. I suppose I couldn't."

"Good to know." He grabs his fork and digs into his salad.

Is Jaxson Masters flirting with me?

No, that's insane.

We spend the next forty minutes eating and chatting like old friends. I'm answering as many questions as I'm asking, and I don't mind one bit. I don't know what it is about him, but he is easy to talk to. You know how—too rarely in life—you meet that one person who you feel you've known your entire existence?

That's him.

Yes, he's hot, but he's also nice and if it wasn't for his brother co-sponsoring whatever charity they decide on, I'd say we could sign up Jaxson for anything and he would rock it with compassion.

He's an easygoing, amenable kind of guy.

I have noticed that he seems to talk about his brother as little as possible, which I suppose is for the best. I'll have to meet the man eventually, and I'd rather have no preconceived ideas outside of the ones I already have formed from this conversation.

So far, I'd say Jepson has some unresolved issues, and he takes them out on his brother, which makes my mama bear roar to life. But again... I need to keep an open mind. They are my clients. I'm here to help both of them and I cannot choose favorites.

"Would you go out on a date with me?"

His question has my head snapping up from my cinnamon and sugar churro. "What?"

"Something low-key, like dinner and a movie."

My mouth hangs open. "I can't."

"Why? Do you have a boyfriend?" He frowns.

"No."

"Are you not into men?" He arches his brow.

I roll my eyes. "I'm too old for you."

"What? Of all the excuses you could have given me, that's the lamest one." He grins. "If you are older than me, it's only by a few years and I don't mind."

"I'm Deacon Scott's age."

"No shit?" His eyes trace over me, but he looks anything other than disgusted. "Did you and he, uh—"

"No," I scoff. "We went to the same high school, same graduating class, but that is it."

"Huh. I never would have guessed. That's right, he's engaged to that tattooed chick from his high school. The one on our medical staff."

"That tattooed chick is London Black, and she's my best friend—that's how I got the job with the Rangers, which is another reason I can't go out on a date with you."

"That's a more passable reason than *I'm too old for you*." He stares at me for a minute. "Okay, how about dinner as friends?"

"You want to be my friend?"

"Yeah, I really do. I like you. You're easy to talk to. So, if you won't go out with me, you can at least be my friend."

"I don't know if I'm allowed to be your friend."

"Who's going to tell?"

I shrug. "These things have a way of coming out."

He sighs. "Would you at least give me your phone number?"

"You already have my phone number." I elbow him softly.

"Nah," He pulls my card out of his pocket. "Not your work number, your real number."

I wrap my fingers around his forearm. "That is my real number. It's a temporary office, so I used my google number which goes straight to my phone."

He raises his brow and pulls out his phone, texting the number on the card. My phone beeps in my purse, which makes him smile. "Should we go back to your hot office?"

I glance at my watch. "The HVAC guy should be here in an hour."

"Do you know the guy they're sending?" He stands and turns to me as I scoot across the vinyl booth.

"No. The building is sending him."

He offers me his hand and helps me to my feet. "Then I'll wait with you until he's done."

That is so sweet and kind of sexy. "I don't want to monopolize your day."

"I can either spend the afternoon talking with my new friend or go home and play Xbox. I'd much rather spend my time talking to you." He tosses a hundred-dollar bill on the table with the check and slides his hand on the small of my back, escorting me out of the restaurant.

I don't know what to say. He's too sweet to say no to and, frankly, I would appreciate the company.

"Can I ask you a question?" I ask as I pull my keys out of my pocket to unlock the front door.

"Yeah, sure." Jaxson pulls it open.

"Exactly how old are you?"

He grins. "Should I lie and tell you I'm older than I am?"

"No, because I would catch you, eventually. Besides, you wouldn't lie to your friend, would you?"

We walk to the back of the room, but instead of retaking our positions around the desk, Jaxson takes charge and rearranges our chairs, propping them up against the wall with the fan pointed at them. Then he grabs two more chairs and puts them in front as footstools. He motions for me to take a seat and then sits beside me with his feet propped up, the fan blowing cool air over us.

"No, I wouldn't lie to you," he says, his big muscular arms crossed over his wide chest. I bet he looks amazing without a shirt on.

Dammit, that is such an inappropriate thought to be bouncing around in my head.

"I turned twenty-seven a few months ago."

"Wow," I muse. "To be twenty-seven again."

He shrugs. "It's not so great."

I giggle and shake my head. "Yeah, I didn't enjoy my twenties all that much, but I never was a partier, so I spent a lot of it in school or fulfilling clinical hours."

He drops his legs and moves to the other seat so he's facing me, his back to the fan. Then he surprises me by pulling my chair forward, my shorter legs allowing us to sit closer. He keeps talking as if he didn't put us within touching distance. "Clinical hours? What's that?"

Although my heart races, I pretend like I'm unaffected by his bold move. "Originally, I went to school to be a therapist."

"Ah. That explains why you're so easy to talk to."

"Actually, people have always found me easy to talk to. I don't know why, but people feel they can open up to me. I'm also not judgmental and I keep an open mind with people. Or at least I try to."

"Why are you not a therapist today?" He rests his hand on my shin and part of me wants to point out that this is not how new friends act. The other part of me doesn't want to deter him. Oh my, I cannot date a man so much younger than me and definitely not a man who plays for the Rocky Mountain Rangers.

"I find it hard not forming an attachment to people, feeling their pain, or harboring their emotions. For my sanity, I thought it was better to find something else to do with my time that could both help people and protect my mental health."

Jaxson stares down at his hand wrapped around my lower leg, his finger still. He doesn't massage or try to move up toward my knee. I guess he is grounding himself via this simple touch. And in some ways, he's grounding me, too. "And now you're helping big, dumb football players be the best versions of themselves by taking care of others."

I lean forward and lay my hand on his, flashing him a big smile. "That's the idea. Although, I haven't met one dumb football player yet."

His blue eyes sparkle. "Oh, just wait. They're coming."

Chuckling, my eyes trail over his soft lips, square jawline, and beguiling dimples. This is a man I could fall for. Nice, attractive and sensitive—add in dominant in the sheets and we have a winner.

I jump when the HVAC guy smacks the metal frame of the doorway with an armful of boxes as he wrestles with the glass door.

"Whew! It's hot in here," Joe Hyland stands there with a tool bag slung over his shoulder, his arms full. Not only did we go to high school together, but he was a football player and spends his evenings at the bar retelling his glory days. He's also a huge jerk who tormented my best friend, London Black, our sophomore, junior and senior years. I can't stand him, and suddenly I'm beyond grateful to Jaxson for staying behind. "Hey! It's Maryanne Merryweather. How are you doing?"

I must stiffen because Jaxson picks up on it, patting my leg before standing tall, his size threatening without speaking a word.

Hyland is oblivious to how he makes others uncomfortable. He always has been. I suppose when he's not drinking, he's passable as a human being, but put a couple of drinks in him and he's a complete asshat.

London's words, but I full-heartedly agree with her.

I sigh and stand. "Hi, Joe. Are you here to fix the A/C?"

"Yep." His eyes bounce between me and Jaxson. "I've been out here before, so I brought a couple of parts with me, as I think I know what the problem is. Give me twenty minutes and I'll have cool air blowing soon."

I'm pretty sure if Jaxson wasn't standing beside me as a silent mountain of intimidation, Joe would have said something inappropriate, as is his way. Instead, he keeps his mouth shut.

Another blessing to my day.

Twenty-five minutes later, there is cold air blowing. He stares at Jaxson as he packs up his tools. "Do I know you?"

Jaxson shakes his head. "Doubt it."

"You're a Ranger, aren't you?"

"I am." Jaxson glances at me, judging my mood. Joe Hyland, while I think he is a jerk, has never been overly nice or mean to me. That's par for the course of my life. I'm someone who seems to get along with everyone just well enough to be liked, but not treasured. Included as part of the crowd, but never a standout. London says it's a blessing and I suppose she's right, although it would be nice to be someone's entire world just once in my life.

"Yeah, I used to play ball with Deacon. We had a lot of good times back then."

That's bullshit. Deacon Scott didn't party with Joe or any of the other football players.

"That's great," Jaxson says without a hint of friendliness.

"What position do you play?"

Jaxson blows out a steady breath, letting it be known to all that he's exercising patience. "I'm a jammer on special teams."

"Oh." Joe seems to get the hint. "Well, I'll be looking for you next Sunday. I'll send the bill to the building owner, Maryanne. See you around,"

We watch as he leaves the building. Then Jaxson breaks the silence with, "What a joke."

"You are very perceptive. He is a joke," I giggle and shake my head.

"Yeah, I guess I read people fairly well." He shoves his hands in his pockets. "Are you done for the day?"

I glance around my office, knowing I should spend another couple of hours here completing all the work I didn't get to today and yet have no motivation to do so. "I could be."

"Want to have dinner?"

"I'm still stuffed from lunch, but I could go for a drink if you're hungry."

"I'm always hungry. I try to eat five or six times a day."

I button up my sweater and then dip into my office to grab my purse. I told him I couldn't date him and he accepted that. So why does this feel like a date? And why am I going along with it?

"Where are we going?"

Chapter Three
Jepson

Jaxson Jeffers Masters—born eleven minutes after me—is technically my baby brother, and yet he's been watching over me for nearly a decade. I never asked him to and sometimes I resent how much more mature and emotionally stable he is than me.

I know I'm a dick sometimes.

I know it, but I can't seem to stop once I'm on a roll. It's almost like I feel everyone looking at me and thinking it, so I can't back down and admit they are right out of sheer pride, no matter how detrimental it is to my reputation. Most of the time, while my mouth and actions are solidifying everyone's opinion of me, on the inside I'm screaming *"What the fuck are you doing? Knock it off!"*

But I don't. Or I can't. Not sure which one it is.

My brother walks on eggshells around me, and I resent him for that, too. I wish he'd tell me to fuck off. I really do. Stand up to me, call me on my shit boldly and then bitch slap me into tomorrow.

But he won't. Or he can't. Again, I'm not sure which one it is.

The garage door opens, causing me to look up from the TV playing the game reel our special teams coordinator uploaded to the cloud for us to review for next week's game. "Where have you been?"

It's nearly eight o'clock at night, which is late for my rule-following brother.

"Uh—" he tosses his keys on the counter and kicks off his shoes "—I was hanging out with Maryanne Merryweather. The A/C in the building was out and some unknown HVAC guy was coming to work on it, and I didn't want her to be alone with a stranger after hours."

I narrow my eyes, interest and suspicion swirling in my brain. "That was nice of you. What is she like?"

He shrugs, plopping down on the chair next to the sofa. "She's nice. Smart. Knows her shit about charities and all that."

"Was she wearing a cat hair-covered cardigan?" I snicker.

He nods. "Actually, she was wearing a sweater."

"I knew it. Did I call it or what?"

"You're a genius. How'd it go with Crystal?" He changes the subject.

"Oh, man. Complete dud," I hit pause on the game footage.

"Seriously? I thought she was going to be a delightful afternoon of stress relief?"

"Me, too. Turns out, Crystal is truly heartbroken over her separation. I guess she and this guy have been together since high school. He was her first and only and she's devastated her marriage is over. We spent the afternoon talking about it. She cried on my shoulder for an hour, and then I left before my inner douchebag could get loose."

Dr. Jekyll and Mr. Hyde—me and my inner asshole fight for control hourly.

Jaxson raises his brow. "You didn't make a move?"

I sigh. "No. I don't know what's wrong with me or where this conscientious bullshit is coming from, but I don't like it. I think you're rubbing off on me."

"It only took twenty-seven years."

"Yeah," I eyeball him. "So, should I swing by the charity chick's place tomorrow and sign some paperwork or something?"

"No." He pulls a folded piece of paper out of his back pocket and tosses it to me. "Fill this out, and I'll work with her to narrow down our choices to three charities. Then we can discuss it."

Son of a bitch. My brother is a shitty liar. "Why don't you want me to meet her?"

His eyes snap up to meet mine. "Why do you suddenly want to meet her?"

I grin. "Because you don't want me to."

Jaxson sighs and shakes his head. "You're the one who didn't want to meet the cat-loving, cardigan-wearing charity chick. I'm saving you the time and her the discomfort. Do what you want."

I watch him as he walks away—acting like he doesn't care when I know he does. We share a house because I don't know why. I don't know why he stays close when I so often do things to push him away. I honestly don't deserve his love and protection, but I'll never tell him that.

I glance through the list of questions. This reads like a dating profile questionnaire and has a head-shrink vibe to it. Why would she need to know about my relationships with my parents, pets, or kids? What does that matter when it comes to raising money for a *worthy* cause?

Whatever her motivation, she certainly snagged my brother's interest today. No matter how hard he tries to hide it, he's protective of her, which means I have to meet her. Could he have a thing for an old cat lady? We never have been attracted to the same women, but I figured that was mostly because Jaxson looks deeper than me.

Yes, I'm a pig. I know this, too.

Although, my actions today were anything but piggish. Today with Crystal, I really felt for her. My heart broke for her. And I wished I could take away her pain by doing something selfless, like getting her and her husband back together. I wonder if he'd hear me out, or if my approach would only make things between them worse.

Jesus Christ! Who the fuck is in my head right now?

Turning off the TV, I toss the remote on the cushion next to me and gather my water bottles and dirty dishes, dumping them in the kitchen before climbing the stairs to my room. Tomorrow is an early day, and spending time in my head today has been utterly exhausting.

Besides, for the next few weeks, I need to give two

hundred percent on the field, reminding the coaches why they recruited me. I sense I'm on the verge of being fired, and I need to be that much better to counteract my shenanigans off the field.

Again—I know this about myself.

How can someone so self-aware be so self-destructive at the same time?

"We are partying tonight!" Rex calls across the locker room. He's joined by a series of hoots and hollers.

"Strip club!" I bellow before I can think better of it. It's only the third game of the regular season, but we played fantastically today. The entire team is in sync. I'm a gunner on special teams, and I stuffed New York's Nelson Jacobs three times on punt returns, resulting in a loss of yards.

I was a special teams god today.

My brother, who plays my opposing position as a jammer, also had a great day on the field and created massive holes for our punt returner, Washburne, which resulted in two touchdowns.

"You got us kicked out of the last strip club, remember?" Rex says.

"That was in Nashville. We have a dozen other cities to be kicked out of this year. Besides, the ladies at Diamonds and Pearls love me." The words fly out of my mouth, even though I know this is the exact image I'm supposed to stop selling.

I smack Jaxson on the shoulder, his locker two stalls away from mine. "What do you think? Want to head up to Denver tonight?"

Part of me hopes he'll say no. Then I'll have a reason to back out of my boldly declared plans for the evening. Although, I genuinely like the ladies at Diamonds and Pearls. I've been there enough times and have had plenty of genuine conversations with many of the dancers. I know about their lives: their names, hometowns, kids and even their pets' names. We've talked about what they are going to school for—if they are going to school—and what their dreams are for after they are no longer dancing. Some of them use their job as a means to an end. Some of them truly love dancing every night and could give a fuck less what people think about how they make their cash. I find most of them fascinating, multi-faceted, confident and empowered women who also are nice to look at. Sometimes I get to know their boyfriends or husbands, and we shoot the shit over a couple of beers, talking football and life in general.

Unlike my conduct in Nashville—or any other strip club in any other town that is not my own—I behave myself with the ladies in my own backyard.

Contrary to popular opinion, I've never dated or fucked one dancer in Denver. Of course, I'll never admit that to the guys. Let them think what they want.

"I don't know, Jeps. I'm not feeling it tonight, you know?" my brother says.

"Why? We just played a phenomenal game. Don't you want to celebrate?" Even though he gives me the answer I secretly want, I still have to push the subject.

I really am that asshole.

"Yeah! *Celebrate good times, come on*," Rex comes between us wearing a towel, singing Kool and the Gang's famous song while swinging his arms and ass before he hip-checks Jaxson into his locker.

"Watch it, stupid ass." Jaxson shoves him back, his smile giving away his good humor.

Greg McMillen, the offensive coordinator, makes his voice boom over the baritone cacophony permeating the locker room. "No one leaves until the coach and the GM talk to you. Rex, do you hear me?"

"Yeah, Coach," Rex grumbles beside me, bringing his arms down.

"I wonder what's going on?" I say under my breath and nod in Aggie's direction as he gets dressed at his locker. He's been through some shit lately, but right now, he looks like he got kicked in the nuts.

Jaxson shakes his head. We've all heard the shit about his soon-to-be ex-wife. "Can't be good."

"Shit." I grab my toiletries and jump in and out of the shower, joining the rest of the team as we wait for our coach and the GM, Mr. Daniel Scott. We don't have to wait long before Mike Monroe and Daniel Scott walk in, followed by Deacon and Declan Scott—the whole fam-damily minus their sister, Deidre, who most of us have never met in person.

Declan, our star quarterback, takes residence center

stage, halfway between his family and his team, with his arms crossed over his chest, his feet spread in a wide stance.

"Listen up," Deacon Scott's voice booms, shutting everyone up.

His father, our GM, Daniel, steps forward and speaks. "You played a great game today and I don't want to diminish this win, but it's early in the season and we still have a long way to go. Unfortunately, there are antics by members of this team overshadowing what should be our championship season. I see no reason to point out anyone specific, as we are a team. We win as a team and we lose as a team. One person's negative actions are the team's bad press."

Fuck me. I don't have to look around to feel the eyes on me. I mean, I'm not the only fuck up, but I'm definitely in the top ten. Last week Wyatt got a DUI and now he's on the inactive list. Before the season, we lost a third-string defensive lineman. Publicly, they let him go because the team didn't need him and he was at the end of his contract, but the rumor is he was fucking Aggie's wife and the organization doesn't play that shit. I'm not sure Aggie knows about that. We're not that close, and I'm not stupid enough to bring up the topic with him.

The GM continues, "Club brawls, DUIs, personal dramas—these take away focus from what matters this season. Record-breaking stats and team cohesion. Since partying and reckless activities seem to be just as important to some of you as winning, I'm imposing a curfew on the team, as well as a gag order with the press, effective immediately. The only sanctioned interviews from members of this team will be coordinated by the President of Communications, Ms. Deidre Scott. Am I understood?"

A murmur of yeses filters through the men assembled.

Mike Monroe steps up. "Until I say otherwise, practice, travel and games will be from seven am to seven pm, Wednesday through Monday. Curfew is on your honor at eight pm. Fuck around and I find out and we'll be discussing your future with the team. Next Wednesday, we will start in the briefing room, where I will discuss a couple of roster changes for the upcoming weeks. Your coaches are going to be pushing you hard to wring the absolute best out of each of you. If all goes well, you'll be too fucking tired for shenanigans."

I swear his eyes land on me with that last word.

"Great game today. Be proud of yourselves, but be prepared for a few brutal weeks as we gear up for our toughest matchup this season against Seattle in week eight. Dismissed."

The locker room is silent until the coaches, the GM and both of the Scotts leave and only then are there low rumbles of dissent amongst the players. Feeling like there is a target painted on my back, I keep my mouth shut and slide my wallet and keys into my pocket. "Pizza and Xbox tonight?"

Jaxson and Rex nod, the three of us exiting the locker room as quickly as possible.

Early the next morning, I hear Jaxson humming to himself in the kitchen. My hair tousled, I wipe the sleep out of my eyes and stumble down the stairs. "What are you doing up?"

Most teams have something every day of the week except for Tuesdays, which is the only pseudo-mandated day off in the league. If they aren't at a game or traveling for a game, they are in the briefing room going over game tapes, on the practice field running drills, in the gym working out, or with medical getting physical therapy. The Rangers, as one of the few family-owned teams left in the league, usually gives us Mondays off too if the team is doing well and we don't have a game. Of course, the coach revoked that shit yesterday, so I'm guessing this is our last two-day weekend for the next couple of months.

Jaxson looks up from the smoothie he's blending. "I'm meeting the charity chick at her office to go over the options she's found for us."

"We have an appointment today?"

My brother sighs. "Yeah, ten o'clock."

I frown. "Were you going to tell me about it?"

"Honestly, no."

"Why not?"

"She's a nice woman and I don't want you insulting her or something."

I slide my hand down my face, tamping down my

frustration. "Look, Jaxs. I'm in enough trouble right now. The last thing I'm going to do is jeopardize my spot on the team by pissing off the charity chick. I need to go to this meeting, get involved and put my pretty face on a couple of billboards or something—preferably with you and the Rangers logo tattooed all over us. Okay?"

He nods. "Okay, but you'll have to drive yourself. I have an errand to run beforehand."

"Okay," I watch as he carries his smoothie up the stairs to his room, leaving the blender soaking in the sink. He never leaves dirty dishes behind.

Interesting.

I roll into the charity chick's office at nine forty-five, figuring I'll catch Jaxson here early, preparing her for his big, bad, asshole brother. Only, his car isn't here. Walking through the front door, an electronic bell dings overhead, alerting her to my arrival.

"Hey you," she calls from her hiding place.

A beautiful, stacked brunette walks out of her office wearing a flirty sundress with a sweetheart neckline, showcasing her ample curves. "Well, hello there."

She stumbles over her feet and approaches with her hand out. "Oh, sorry. I thought you were Jaxson. You must be Jepson."

"I must be." My eyes trail over her unapologetically. "Who are you?"

"I'm Maryanne." She waits for me to acknowledge her name and take her hand. When I don't, she frowns. "Merryweather."

A dark chuckle escapes my lips, and I shake my head. "No, you're not."

"Yes, I am." She glances over my shoulder at the door.

"Not possible."

"Why not?"

"Because you are way too hot to be a cat-loving, cardigan-wearing charity chick."

"Oh," she frowns, her brain processing my words. "Wait, what?"

I walk a slow circle around her, checking out every inch of her lush body. She's a little thicker than I'm normally attracted to, but her curves are drool-worthy and her face has that sweet innocence of the girl next door begging to be dirtied up a bit. The type of dirtying I would volunteer for. "You really are her? No wonder my brother didn't want me to meet you."

"Why wouldn't he want you to meet me? Are you a big jerk or something?"

I smile. She's feisty and I like it. "Compared to him, yeah."

She takes a step back and leads me to a table on the other side of the room. "Well, he is a nice guy."

"What about you, Maryanne? Are you a *nice* girl?" I follow her, my eyes glued to the sway of her hips. Fuck me, she's gorgeous, smart and snarky.

Glancing over her shoulder, she rolls her eyes. "I'm too nice for someone like you."

"I don't think that's true. I enjoy nice. Somebody nice is exactly what I need in my life." I flash her my Sunday school smile when she stops and turns to face me.

She laughs. "Do you always come onto women like this?"

"Not all women." I offer her my hand, completing the handshake I fucked up earlier, but before I let go, I lift her fingers to my lips and press a wholesome kiss to her soft, fragrant skin.

"Where's Jaxson?" She narrows her eyes and pulls her hand from mine, reminding me to behave myself.

That rat bastard—trying to hide her from me and keep her for himself.

I shrug, taking a step back and sliding my hands into my pockets. "I thought he'd be here already."

"Well, I guess you and I can get acquainted while we wait. Would you like some coffee or water?" She motions for me to take a seat.

"Water would be great. Thank you." I watch as she walks away, my body hardening in all the right and some of the oh-so-wrong ways. I've never been instantly smitten with a woman before, not just lusting after her body, but intrigued by her personality. If Jaxson thought he could keep her from me, he has another *think* coming. He'll claim this is basic sibling rivalry—my need to covet everything he wants. I will admit, usually I do it just to fuck with him. To see if he'll back down and give whatever it is to me without a fight.

This is not one of those moments.

Chapter Four
Maryanne

Obviously, as an identical twin, I knew Jepson Masters would be attractive, but he has this raw sexuality and confidence radiating off his skin that Jaxson tones down. Within thirty seconds of meeting Jepson, I feel stripped bare, licked and caressed and left panting for more.

And he did that with just his eyes.

Jaxson might look like a bad boy, but Jepson is the naughty Ned that smart girls like me are supposed to know better than to fall for. He's a break-your-heart and bed-frame kind of guy—no doubt in my mind.

"Here." I hand him a bottle of water, setting a second one down for when Jaxson arrives.

"Thank you."

"I think Jaxson and I covered the basics. I have five charities for you to look at today, but maybe you want to tell me a bit about yourself first?" Sitting across from him,

I lean back in my chair. Part of me wants to put on a sweater. I'm fully aware of how big chested I am and I only wore this flirty little dress today because I thought it was going to be just me and Jaxson—the guy I know I shouldn't be flirting with and yet haven't been able to stop thinking about since meeting last week. Of course, receiving good morning and sleep well texts every day hasn't helped me get him out of my mind either.

On the other hand, I know if I put on a sweater now, Jepson will know it's because of him and think he won.

Guys like him turn everything into a challenge or battle of wills.

Plus, he called me a cat-loving, cardigan-wearing charity chick.

What the hell is that?

"What would you like to know?" He cracks the bottle and takes a deep drink, his throat working as he gulps half the bottle.

I wouldn't think watching a man's Adam's apple could be so seductive.

I was wrong.

"Well, I'm not sure. Your brother said you are a private person, so I'm not sure what is appropriate to ask."

Jepson sits back in his seat and crosses his ankle over his knee—a genuine power pose. "Did he? What else did he tell you about me?"

I shrug. "Not a lot. Everything I know about you, I learned online after he and I met."

"Oh god, I shudder to think what you've read about me online," He grins and I have to guess he's gotten out of as much trouble as he's gotten into with that smile.

"You frequent gentlemen's clubs and seem to get kicked out of them, often," I blurt, my shrewd gaze waiting for a reaction.

He sighs, not giving me the reaction I'm expecting. I thought maybe he'd puff up and tell me how much exotic dancers love him, but he looks a tad embarrassed. "That happened twice, and both times had nothing to do with the dancers. Could you not find anything else about me online?"

"I didn't dig deep. I prefer to interview in person and form my own opinions versus reading what others think."

"That's generous of you. And while I am a fairly private person about my family, for you, I'm a wide-open book. You can ask me anything, although I'd prefer to hear about you."

Pressing my lips together, I lean back in my chair. "What would you like to know?"

"Do you like to dance?"

"What kind of dance?" I arch my brow.

"Any kind of dance. Club, hip-hop, tap, ballet, the mambo, the flamenco—" he grins "—Zumba. Anything that requires you to swing your hips."

"I dance around in my living room, but I'm not much for going out."

"That's too bad. I would love to see you move your body on the dance floor."

I roll my eyes and shake my head, something I think I'm going to be doing a lot with him, but I can't stop the smile from spreading across my lips. "Is there anyone you won't flirt with?"

"Yes." He doesn't expand his thought process. "Maybe you and I can go out dancing sometime. Hell, I'll even take a ballroom dancing lesson if that's what you want to do."

"I'm tempted to say yes just so you have to dance the waltz."

His grin widens. "Is next week too soon for you?"

Who am I right now? What lucky star did I stumble under that I have a new job that pays well and I really enjoy, as well as being in a position where hot guys flirt with me?

Not just flirt, but actively pursue me. It's like I won the lottery in hot, young, unavailable men.

I shake my head. "I can't."

"Why not?"

"Because we're working together," *And I'm way too old for you and your brother already asked me out.* I think, with no intention of saying it out loud. I wonder if Jaxson told him about me?

Considering how neither brother seems to include their twin in the conversation, I'm betting the answer is no.

He rolls his eyes back at me. "Lame. I thought you were going to hit me with something like I'm too old for you."

I laugh. "Actually, I am older than you."

"Nice. I've always wanted to date an older woman."

"Are you into older women?"

He shrugs. "I've never given it much thought. I like beautiful women and you, Maryanne, are beautiful inside and out."

"You don't know that," I challenge him with a raise of my brow. "I could be a cat-torturing, parka-wearing, serial killer."

"I was wondering if that was going to come back to bite me in the ass."

I giggle. "How do you feel?"

"Bitten. But as long as you're the one doing the biting, I don't mind."

I can't help it—I'm charmed by him. I can't imagine anyone who wouldn't be. "You have a comeback for everything, don't you?"

"Not everything."

I giggle again. "I feel like you're challenging me to stump you."

He quirks his left eyebrow. "Give me your best shot."

I want to ask about his relationship with Jaxson, considering in a moment of vulnerability last week he mentioned Jepson hates him. Does he and if so, why? Why maintain contact, live in the same city, play for the same team, or live in the same house if you hate each other?

"Do you enjoy having a twin brother?"

He shrugs. "Most of the time, it's cool. Sometimes it's not."

"Why is that?"

"Imagine being forced to look in the mirror, even when you don't want to. I assume it's the same as anybody has with any sibling. Sometimes when you look at them, you have reminders of the past that you'd rather forget. What about you? Do you have any siblings?"

"I have a younger brother, but he's significantly younger. He's closer to your age than he is mine."

Just saying it out loud makes me realize how young these guys are. My brother is twenty-six, and he's already married with a kid.

"Have you started receiving AARP applications in the mail yet?"

I giggle again. Something about Jepson makes me giddy. "I'm not that old."

"Then I don't see a problem."

"Why do you think young guys want to date older women? I mean, I look at the two of us and I'm pretty sure you have way more experience than I do. So, it can't be that."

"I don't fetishize dating older women. However, in your case, I see no reason for your age to deter me from wanting to get to know you better. As I said, you are beautiful inside and out. So why would I care how old you are?"

Well, it looks like he stumped me instead.

"What do you say, Maryanne? Want to have dinner with me tonight?"

"She can't." Jaxson walks in behind us. Did the electronic bell ding, and I missed it?

Jepson turns to look at his brother. "Why not?"

"Because she's having dinner with me."

Jepson's smile widens as he swings his eyes back to me. "Really? You two have a date tonight?"

"It's not a date," I say at the same time that Jaxson says, "Yes, we do."

"Isn't this interesting? One of you thinks it's a date, the other thinks it's—what? Two friends going out for a meal?" Jepson shrugs. "Okay. Tomorrow night, Maryanne, you and I will have a *not-a-date* dinner."

I have quickly lost control of this situation and the dynamics of this exchange. And while I enjoy flirting with Jepson, I can feel the tension radiating off these two.

Time to diffuse.

I stand with my hands up. "I'm not sure what is going on here, but this is getting out of hand."

"There's nothing out of hand," Jepson flashes us an easy smile. He looks relaxed as he leans back in his chair with his arm draped over the edge of the table.

"Is this a sibling rivalry thing?" I glance between them. While Jepson looks at ease, Jaxson is definitely on edge. The last thing I want to do is upset him or cause problems between them.

"No." Jepson shakes his head and pats the seat next to him. "I didn't know Jaxs had asked you out when I did... so this is not a rivalry thing."

"Can I talk to you outside?" Jaxson pulls the second chair away from Jepson and takes a step back.

"I..." oh shit. Shit, shit, shit. What do I do here? On any given Sunday, I barely garner one man's attention and never two.

"It's okay, Maryanne. We're fine," Jepson says calmly as he stands. "Give me and my brother five minutes and then we can go over the charities you've chosen for us. Right, Jaxs?"

Jaxson nods. "Five minutes."

Chapter Five
Jaxson

Jepson leans his ass against my car, crossing his arms over his chest. "You sneaky little fucker. You thought you could keep me away from her by letting me believe she's some old hag."

"I said nothing of the sort. I just didn't correct you when you went on about it."

He nods. "Yeah, I suppose that is on me. Even so, you were trying to keep me from meeting her."

"Yeah, because I knew you would make a move on her just to spite me."

"This isn't about you. She's everything you said she was and more. Nice, smart, snarky, and fucking gorgeous." He shrugs. "Of course, I'm going to ask her out."

I pace a six-foot section in front of him, my anger rising the calmer he seems.

What is this opposite day? He's usually the one on the verge of blowing a gasket and I'm the one trying to calm him down, not vice versa. "You expect me to back down like I always do, but not this time, Jepson. I'm not letting you have your way, and I'm not giving you what you want. I already have a date with her—"

"Do you though? There seems to be some confusion about whether this is a date." He flashes a taunting grin.

I narrow my eyes. "It's a fucking date. She's worried about calling it that because we're working together, and she has this hang-up about being older than us."

Jepson's grin turns into a full-blown smile. "Us. Not you, but us."

"Fuck off," I grumble.

He chuckles. "Calm down, man. I don't expect you to back down. As a matter of fact, I'm proud of you for standing your ground. I'll admit I have fucked with you in the past, simply because I want to see if you'll let me have my way—which you always do—but I'm thrilled you're not going to now. However, I'm not backing down either."

I shake my head. "You are impossible."

He holds his hands up and pulls his ass off the fender of my BMW. "Hear me out. We're both interested in getting to know her on a personal level—a very personal level—so we go on a couple of dates and see where things go. Maybe I'll lose interest after one date or maybe you'll change your mind about what you're feeling. Or maybe she won't like either of us and tells us to go fuck ourselves. If you weren't my brother and some other random guy, I would have no problem knowing you were casually seeing the same woman I'm dating. If anything, knowing there's competition out there motivates me to be on my best behavior. So, why should it be any different for us?"

"It is different because we're brothers and we live together and we have a lifetime of sibling rivalry bullshit between us. Plus, you should always be on your best behavior. She deserves nothing less."

"God, you are such a boy scout and I love that about you."

I roll my eyes but say nothing, although I am surprised to hear him say he loves anything about me. We don't come from the most lovey-dovey family. Any warmth died with our mother.

Jepson shrugs. "We've cracked Pandora's box, Jaxs. We met her, we want her and we know it. There's no moving forward that doesn't end in resentment if one of us feels like he has to give up. Let's try this for a couple of weeks and see where it goes."

"We're on lockdown for the next couple of weeks, possibly months." I remind him.

"Even better. It means we take the time to get to know her. No jealousy and no crazy grand gestures, because both of us are going to be insanely busy."

"You're such a dick." I shake my head and shove my hands in my pockets.

"Is that the first thing you're going to tell her about me?" Jepson raises his brow, the first sign of concern crossing his handsome, unblemished face. Of course, Maryanne is attracted to him. My brother, while a first-class dick, can be charming when he wants to be. I bet he rolled in, took one look at her and immediately put the moves on before he even learned her name.

I don't know how early he showed up, or how many minutes they've been chatting and getting to know each other, but I was late picking up a bouquet that is currently sitting in my passenger seat. I had planned to walk in with them, but then I saw his car and knew I was screwed.

I shake my head. "If she agrees to go out with you, she can learn who you are all on her own. She doesn't need to hear any of it from me."

Jepson slaps his palms together and then offers me one. "Deal. No trashing each other."

"She's never going to go for this." I shake my head and his hand.

"You let me do the talking. I'm better at selling the crazy shit, anyway."

We walk into the building to find Maryanne nervously stacking piles of papers in front of our chairs. There are bottles of water and pens placed neatly beside each stack and everything has a lawyer's office sheen to it.

Also, she's wearing her sweater buttoned to the top.

She looks up as we walk in and blurts, "I have to apologize. I allowed things to become unprofessional, and I'm rectifying that right now."

Jepson shakes his head and looks at me with a wry grin on his face.

I sigh. "Everything is cool, Maryanne."

"No," she shakes her head emphatically. "It's not. I'm sorry. You're both very charming and good-looking men, and I allowed the situation to get out of hand, and I should've never flirted with you or allowed you to flirt with me, and that's on me as the professional here, and—"

Jepson laughs at her rambling. "Is this how you handle all men who show an interest in you? Push them away with fears of impropriety?"

I chuckle, feeding off his energy and smacking him on the arm. "Impropriety? Have you been reading historical romances or something?"

He shrugs. "I might've caught a couple of episodes of Bridgerton on Netflix. It's actually really good."

Maryanne's eyes bounce between me and my brother. "You aren't mad?"

We both shake our heads, but as usual, Jepson is the one to talk. "Nope. My brother has good taste and so do I."

"I see." She lets out a big breath. "Well, let's talk about the charities, then."

The three of us sit down and go over pamphlets from five different charities. On the top is the one she recommends the most—a local chapter of the Big Brothers Big Sisters. It makes sense, considering we are co-sponsoring as brothers. She proposes that we host a couple of group events where the kids not only hang out with us and their big brothers, but they meet other kids in similar situations to form supportive bonds with their peers. We would host one event per quarter and could branch out to other charities by having the kids help with something like an adoption fair for the puppy mill rescue.

Her second suggestion is to team up with a new local veteran housing charity called Paladin Place. Considering our father worked in construction building houses in new communities, she thinks we can use our limited skills to bring awareness with a couple of in-person events. Nothing dangerous, but something with a Jimmy Carter meets Habitat for Humanity vibe, except local and specific to homeless veterans.

Then there is the Spring City Shelter, a local homeless shelter and food kitchen. Purrfect Paws Preserve, an animal rescue and rehabilitation. And lastly, Penny's Playground, which is an after-school leadership program for kids.

"This is a lot of information, and I don't expect you to pick one today, but what do you think?" Maryanne has a rosy glow to her cheeks and I can tell that talking about this stuff invigorates her. She's passionate about helping others, which is another thing to love about her.

"Which one do you think would benefit the most from our attention?" I ask.

She shrugs, but with a smile on her face. "They can all use your attention, but in the end, it's important to find something you are passionate about because that will radiate through every word and action you take. Your infectious excitement will incite other people to get involved. Remember, this isn't about you throwing money at something, this is about throwing your energy into a worthy cause."

I glance at my brother. I know which one I'm leaning toward—homes for veterans—but that's mostly because I think it would be fun to work on the houses. We don't have any military in our immediate family, although we grew up near Fort Jackson and so we've had soldiers around us most of our lives. Some of our old friends and classmates are on active duty and our father has a lot of veteran buddies at the bar. "What do you think?"

"From a gimmick perspective, it seems like doing something with the Big Brothers would be the best promotion for the team, but a part of me would love to swing a hammer like Jimmy Carter." Jepson makes a chopping motion with his hand.

"Yeah, that's what I was thinking, too."

"Don't suppose we could do both?" He looks up at her.

Maryanne shakes her head. "That would be a lot of overhead, and I don't think you guys have the time to commit to something like that. However, I plan on presenting Paladin Place to a couple of your teammates, so you could always appear at one of their events and swing a hammer then."

"Good idea." I thumb through the five she gave us again, knowing there are hundreds more she didn't present.

It is nice that there are people out there trying to do good for others.

It's also a somber reminder that there are so many people out there needing help.

"How are you going to organize all of this by yourself?" I asked Maryanne, realizing the amount of work it will take for her to manage our involvement, much less all the other coordination that goes into teaming up with an established charity. What if we had wanted to create our own? How would she handle all of it?

"I'm hiring a team. I interviewed and selected two last week. Soon I will have a staff of four working directly for me." Her grin is wide and a little goofy. "I'm super excited because I've never had a staff that works directly for me. I want to make this a place that people stand in line to apply to."

"That's great," Jepson says.

"I'm sure you're going to be an amazing boss," I add.

"So, what do we do next?" Jepson says, pulling his phone out of his pocket as it beeps with an incoming message.

Maryanne clasps her hands together. "Next, I contact the charity and let them know we have a couple of football players interested in supporting their organization. Then, I'll brainstorm with them a couple of events over the next six months that you guys can promote and attend. Do you have an active social media presence?"

I shake my head at the same time the Jepson grins. "I've been told to tone down my online communications."

She chuckles. "I can only imagine. One of the people I'm hiring is a social media guru, so they will help both of you pump up your online presence and give you a plat-

form where you can promote your charitable contri-
butions."

"Who alerts the organization about what we've
chosen today?" Jepson arches his brow, sliding his phone
back into his pocket.

"I have a bi-weekly meeting with Deidre Scott. I'll let
her know then, and I assume she filters it through the rest
of the organization."

"Outstanding. And what else do you need from us?"
I've been taking my cues from Jepson, as I have most of
my life. We walked in, dismissed her concerns, and
immediately got down to business. But I know him. The
conversation about dating her is not over.

What's he waiting for?

"Have you decided on Big Brothers Big Sisters?" She
raises her brow.

Jepson and I exchange a look and nod. "Sounds like a
winner to us."

"Okay. This is great!" She stands and leans over the
table to grab our papers, her hair falling over her eyes in
front of our faces. I can smell her sweet citrus shampoo
and can't stop myself from inhaling deeply. I glance at
Jepson, noticing him doing the same thing.

Dammit. This isn't simple sibling rivalry, and he isn't
doing this to fuck with me.

He really is interested in her.

For most of our life, I've backed down and given him
what he wants. He was the first out of the womb, first to
pick new clothes—although we both grew so quickly,
hand-me-downs weren't an option—first to drive and first

to date. Before the accident, my parents and I found fighting with him exhausting. Afterward... well, I felt I owed him.

It's my fault he didn't have time to say goodbye to our mother. I mean, logically I know it is not my fault. I was fourteen with a bleeding ulcer and acute pancreatitis. I wasn't driving the car or the eighteen-wheeler and although we wrecked because of me, everything was an accident.

And yet, I can't shake the responsibility weighing on my shoulders. Jepson has never openly blamed me, but his unwillingness to talk about it points the finger in my direction every time.

Same with our father.

So, I've willingly let him have his way—penance for sins of the past.

But I'm tired of holding myself back, only doing a smidge under his best, making sure I never overshadow him. Something tells me the roster changes the coach plans to announce on Wednesday include moving me up from second-string cornerback to first-string, and if it pisses Jepson off, so be it. I won't trash him to Maryanne, but if she picks me over him, so be that, too.

Coach Monroe is right. I need to think about my future, and I'm thinking Maryanne could be a part of it.

As if she can hear the thoughts in my head—or maybe she hears me sniffing her hair—she glances up through her lush auburn locks with a light blush on her cheeks. "Sign here."

Our eyes connect and I'm transported to last week

when it was just her and me talking, flirting, and laughing while spending an impromptu day together. I flash her a gentle smile and take the pen, signing on the dotted line.

What did I sign? I don't have a clue.

"What are we signing?" Jepson interjects.

She breaks eye contact with me and smiles at him, handing him the pen. "It's a simple intent to sponsor, promote and support the named charity on behalf of yourself and the Rangers Football Organization. It's not legally binding, just a show of good faith. I'll take these to Deidre, where she keeps them on file as part of your employment and endorsement contracts."

Jepson takes the pen, signs and hands it back to her. "Cool. Are we done with the business at hand?"

"Yes." She grabs the papers and pulls back. "You guys are free to go. I'll work on this and get back to you in a couple of weeks with more information."

"Great." Jepson pushes out of his chair and stretches his arms over his head, throwing a smirk in my direction, which usually means trouble. "You two have a great dinner tonight, and Maryanne, I'll pick you up tomorrow. We have an eight o'clock curfew, so can you get out of here before five?"

Yep. Bull in a china shop. That's my brother Jepson.

I turn my attention to her to gauge her reaction.

Her mouth drops open. "No. I thought we resolved this. I can't date either of you."

"Why not?" Damn him, he sounds genuinely confused.

"I..." She glances between us, quickly losing the

battle. I'd laugh if I hadn't been on the receiving end of Jepson's rationale myself. My brother is running with this, so I keep my expression blank. He's not wrong. If anyone can sell this crazy idea to her, it's him. It's mind-boggling how good of a salesman he is. Damn guy could sell ice to a polar bear.

Jepson counts on his fingers. "One—we met, talked, flirted, and still got business done, so being professional isn't a good excuse. Two—I don't give a fuck how old you are and neither does Jaxson, so that's not an excuse. And three—you are attracted to us, and we are very interested in you, so why not get to know us and see where this goes?"

"You would be okay with me dating your brother?"

He nods.

She swings her eyes to me. "And you are okay with me dating him?"

I shrug. "I'm not bothered by it. At least with him, I know who my competition is."

Jepson walks around the table and places his hands on her upper arms, turning her to face him. He slides a finger under her chin and tilts her head back, so she has no choice but to look into his eyes.

I feel like I should be jealous, but I'm fascinated by the control and care with which he handles her.

"I know this seems crazy—and maybe it is—but if we're okay with it, shouldn't you be too? We're not asking for your hand in marriage, just a couple of dates to get to know each other. That's all."

"A couple of dates?" She quirks her brow.

"Three or four tops. If you're not sick of me by then, we'll renegotiate." He gives her his Sunday school smile.

She says nothing.

He swipes his thumb across her bottom lip and takes a step back before winking and releasing her. "Have a nice dinner. I'll text you tomorrow."

Still stuck in some stupor—one I understand because I've been railroaded by Jepson before—she stands there as my brother claps hands with me and walks out the door.

Chapter Six
Maryanne

"What the hell just happened?" I say out loud to anyone who will answer.

Jaxson chuckles. "You've met Jepson Jessup Masters. He's not a man who takes no for an answer."

I raise my brow. "And you are?"

"I approach the word no a bit differently than him."

"Are you really okay with this?"

He shrugs. "My brother made some good points outside. The resentment between us if one of us has to back down will be significantly worse than playing this out and seeing where it goes."

"I don't want to cause problems between the two of you."

"You're not." Jaxson grabs my hand and pulls me around the table to stand in front of him. Like Jepson did, he pulls me close enough to be intimate while crossing no unspoken boundaries. "Think of it this way—what if you had two guys ask you out a day apart from each other?

Would you tell the second guy no because you were in a committed relationship?"

"I rarely have one guy ask me out, much less two."

"I don't understand why."

I shrug, casting my eyes down and biting my lip under his scrutiny. When we hung out last week, he would look at me like he is now—with desire bubbling under the surface. There were many times that I thought, this is it, he's going to kiss me. But he didn't do anything other than a peck on my cheek and a brush of his lips against my knuckles. He has amazing self-control, and I'm terrified of making a fool of myself.

Plus, until this moment, I kept telling myself that this is not a date.

I guess, even though I said the words and he verbally agreed, in his mind, it is most certainly a date.

"What time can I pick you up for dinner?" Jaxson gently brushes a lock of hair from my face and then releases my bottom lip from my teeth with a swipe of his thumb, just like his brother did minutes ago.

I stare into his blue eyes. "Do you really have a curfew?"

He smiles sheepishly. "Yeah. Things are a little stressed in the Rangers' camp right now."

"I have two of my new employees coming in for a few hours to train, but I think I can get out of here by four." I take a step back because otherwise, I'm going to kiss him.

"Okay. I'll pick you up at four-oh-five."

Giggling, I shake my head. "Why don't you pick me

up at my place at four thirty? I'll text you the address. That way, I have a few minutes to freshen up."

"Are you wearing this dress tonight?" He boldly pulls my arms away from my body, making it obvious he's checking me out. "Without the sweater?"

I nod.

"Good. See you tonight." He leans in and kisses my cheek before letting go of my arms and walking out the door. The electronic bell dings as he leaves. I walk into my office and slump into my chair, tingles radiating through my body, their intensity gathering in my breasts and between my legs.

I've been fantasizing about Jaxson for a week, even though I've been denying it. I was looking forward to our dinner tonight, but meeting Jepson has me conflicted. Not about my attraction to Jaxson. He's rough but good-looking, nice, and thoughtful—all the things a girl like me should want. His brother, who is just as hot, is a temptation and invitation to the wild side of my fantasies.

The electronic bell dings again and Jaxson is in my doorway with a beautiful bouquet of pink and white roses. "I got you these so you think about me throughout the day."

I jump out of my chair. "Oh my god, they are beautiful."

"Like you." He winks and leaves without another word.

My two new employees show up at noon to fill out paperwork and review materials. Once I have them set on their tasks, I call my best friend London for advice.

Her dating history isn't much better than mine, but at this point, I need someone to talk to and she's the only one I trust.

She has her own self-made drama going on and beside her and Deacon, I'm the only one who knows it.

Publicly, they announced their impromptu engagement and whirlwind love affair, but I know it's all a ruse to get Deacon the GM position on the team at the end of the season. Ever since reconnecting at our fifteen-year high school reunion, they've been talking daily with a deadline on their fake relationship. London says she's not developing feelings, but I fear I'll be helping her nurse a broken heart when this is all over.

I mean, Deacon is a great guy, so I hope they can both get what they want without hurting each other.

"Hey girl," London chirps upon answering her phone.

I close my door and sigh. "Hey. I feel like I haven't talked to you in forever."

"Well, we both have new jobs with the Rangers, which are super time-consuming. How's it going on your end?"

"Busy. I've hired a staff, two of which started today."

"Oh my god! That's amazing, Maryanne. You deserve all the great things."

"Thanks. How are things going between you and Deacon?"

London sighs. "Why does he have to be a nice guy on top of being hot, rich, and successful? This whole thing would be easier if he was a jerk."

I giggle. "He was always nice."

"Yeah. What's going on with you?"

"Well..." Where do I start? "Have you ever dated two men at the same time?"

"What do you mean?"

"Like, one guy asks you out on Monday and a different guy asks you out on Tuesday. Do you go out with both of them?"

"Are you committed to the Monday guy?"

"No. I mean, we haven't gone out yet, but we've talked quite a bit and I like him a lot. He's sweet, thoughtful, and cute."

"What about the Tuesday guy?"

Now it's my turn to sigh. "He's hot. Sexy and charming, with an alpha vibe to him."

She giggles. "So, you're saying you want to go out with him, too?"

I groan. "How do I date two men without hurting one of them?"

"Well, I think if you're open and honest about everything, then you don't worry about their feelings. Focus on yours."

"That sounds very selfish."

"And? You've spent your entire life taking care of others. Why not be a little selfish? If you have two great guys who want to get to know you, and if they are aware of each other, then have fun."

"How far do I let it go?" Jepson said to give them a couple of dates. I suppose I should know if I want to continue seeing one of them after one or two dates, but what if I don't?

"What do you mean? Are you asking about sex?"

"I can't sleep with them!" I say a little too loud for my flimsy walled office.

"Why not? I mean, if you're trying to figure out how much you like them, isn't gauging your intimacy and sexual compatibility a crucial part of a relationship?"

"I know, but sleeping with two men at the same time?"

"Men do it all the time, Maryanne, so why can't you? Trust me, if the day ever comes that I have two hot, sexy, amazing men vying for my attention at the same time—after Deacon and I end our fake engagement, of course—I will have no problem sleeping with both of them. Again, as long as they know about each other."

"It's so scandalous." A hot blush hits my cheeks as I think about either of them touching me intimately, the tingles from earlier returning tenfold.

"Who's going to know? Except for me because you have to tell me everything. By the way, who are these guys?"

There's a knock on my door, saving me from finishing

this part of the conversation. "Shoot. I have to go, London."

"Okay, but you better call me later."

"I have plans tonight, so it'll be later this week."

"Oh my god. I can't wait," she squeals.

At four twenty-seven, Jaxson pulls up in front of my house and walks across the cracked concrete sideway to my front door.

"Hi." I swing open the door a little too enthusiastically. I spent the last four hours of my day thinking about what London said. They know about each other and they're the ones that came up with this idea, so as long as I'm honest with them about what I'm feeling, it's on them to not let their hearts get broken. This is good because it allows me to focus on my heart and make sure that I am not letting my emotions run away while being seduced by two handsome, well-built, powerful men.

Jaxson looks amazing in a pair of black slacks and a black-and-white striped button-down shirt. He has the cuffs of his sleeves rolled up to the middle of his forearms and the first two buttons undone from his collar, which allow a bit of the tattoos on his chest to peek through.

His heated gaze trails down my body before coming back up to meet mine. "I didn't get to tell you earlier, but you look stunning in this dress."

Blushing, I do a little shimmy to make the skirt flare.

"I wore it for you. It's not something I would normally wear into the office."

He grins. "I like that you wore it for me. Are you ready to go?"

"Yes."

"I thought we'd get Thai food. Do you like it?"

"I love it, and there's a cute little bistro around the corner."

"Yeah, that was the one I was thinking we could go to. Are you up for a walk?" He takes a step back from the threshold.

"That sounds nice." I grab my purse and lock my door behind me, a bit surprised he didn't invite himself into my house.

"How was the rest of your day?" He interlaces his fingers with mine as we walk hand-in-hand the three blocks to the restaurant.

Walking with him feels natural—as if we've known each other forever.

"Busy, but to be honest..." I smile at him. "Something distracted me most of the afternoon."

"Us?" He quirks his brow.

"Yes."

"And what did you decide?"

"We're all adults here and as long as we're being honest with each other, I shouldn't worry about things."

"Exactly." He brings my hand up to his lips and kisses it again. "Jepson and I worked out this afternoon, and it was fine. No drama whatsoever."

"That's good." I search my mind for a new topic, one

that makes this entire situation normal. "Are you an animal lover?"

He chuckles. "I'm a cat guy and a sucker for a big fat, orange tabby, but that might be because I went to Clemson, which is why I have giant cat claw prints on my chest."

"I was going to ask about your tattoos sometime tonight."

"Yeah, I figure with all my scars I might as well get some tattoos too."

"Your scars are from your car accident?"

He nods but doesn't say more as we walk into the restaurant and are greeted by the hostess.

Once we are seated and have ordered our dinners, Jaxson slides his hand on top of my thigh underneath the table. His hand is just high enough to give me ideas, but he doesn't make a move or do anything inappropriate. He just lets it sit there. I like how he seeks comfort in touching me. It makes me feel cherished.

"What about you?" He smiles before taking a sip of his green tea. "Are you a cat or a dog person?"

"I like both. We had one of each growing up and I lost my childhood cat six months ago. She wasn't as tolerant of new dogs after Dixon, my childhood dog, died four years ago, so I couldn't bring another animal into the house. But I've been thinking about getting a kitten and a puppy so they can grow up together."

"One of each," he chuckles, further commentary disrupted by the server.

One thing I love about Thai food, the meals come out

quickly. Within ten minutes, I have hot pad Thai sitting in front of me, and a plate of garlic chicken in front of him. I ordered mine at a level two, which sometimes is a little too hot for me, but Jaxson orders his at a level one which reminds me of his pancreatitis.

"What are the diet concerns for your condition? Do you have to avoid spicy foods?"

"I could eat it occasionally if I loved it, but honestly, I'm a wimp when it comes to hot food. My brother devours it, but I'm not a fan of spice for the sake of burning off my taste buds."

That's the second time he's mentioned Jepson. I wasn't sure if we were going to be avoiding the topic or not. But Jaxson speaks so casually about him, it's like we're talking about an old friend. Before I know it, we're done eating, and he has his hand resting on my thigh again, but now I'm leaning my body against his side and my cheek against his arm as we wait for our check.

"Are you tired?" His breath hits the fine hairs around my face and tickles my cheek. I look up to see his lips so close to mine, it would take nothing to stretch my neck and claim them.

"Not tired, just happy and full."

"Do you want to grab a coffee or a gelato or something? I think I saw something nearby. Damn, I guess I should've driven."

I fix my eyes on his lips and he notices if the way his breath hitches is any sign. I shake my head. "I have ice cream at my house if you want some?"

He nods. "Let's go home."

I'm so deep inside my head that I barely register our walk home. All I focus on is the feel of his thumb as it brushes across the back of my hand repeatedly, the nerves building in my belly and the chant inside of my head. *How far do I let this go? How far do I let this go? How far do I let this go?*

I unlock my door and invite him in, setting my purse and keys down on the hall table. He doesn't let go of my hand and pulls me into his chest as soon as my other hand is free. Leaning against my closed front door, Jaxson places our joined hands on his shoulder while sliding his other hand around my waist and down my back, pulling me flush against him. His body is hard, a wall of well-honed muscle, but the look on his face is tender. He brushes his fingers against my cheek, his thumb against my lips as he lowers his mouth to mine.

His kiss is sweet and tentative, testing my response. Something within me lets go of all of my concerns, my lips parting with the first swipe of his tongue. His lips grow firm, his touch bold, his hand sliding into my hair and pulling my head back to deepen our kiss. I melt into his arms, my hands sliding up his chest to wrap around his neck, his tongue tangling with mine.

I moan, which gives Jaxson all the encouragement he needs. He slides his hands under my ass and lifts me into his arms. On autopilot, I wrap my legs around his waist and let him carry me into the living room. Our mouths remain fused until he sits down on the couch with me straddling his hips. He pulls back and strokes my cheek, a sweet smile on his face. "I've been dreaming about doing that for a week."

"Only a week? I've been dreaming of being kissed like that my whole life."

Jaxson's smile grows as he slides his hand up my thigh under my skirt. "What else have you been dreaming about?"

I suck in my breath, placing my hand on top of his when his thumb brushes the edge of my panties. "I..."

"It's okay, Maryanne. We can go as slow as you need." He doesn't remove his hand but doesn't creep up any higher either, his thumb slowly swiping back and forth as he claims my lips again, removing all words between us.

The problem is, I don't want to go slow. I want to climb him like a tree. But I know as soon as Jepson texts me flirtatious little notes that will no doubt make me blush tomorrow, I'm going to want to go out with him, too. How can I go out with him with fresh memories of Jaxson touching me, caressing me—making me come with his fingers or his mouth or his—

Oh god. I grind down at the same time Jaxson lifts his hips, letting me know exactly what's waiting for me when I'm ready. He continues to kiss me with the kind of passion I've never experienced before. All-consuming, he touches me as if I'm the air he needs to survive right now, with a thin veil of desperation. He kneads my thighs with his strong hands and slides his fingers up my sides and over my breasts before tangling in my hair, only to trail back down again. Whimpering and on the verge of saying *screw it, take me now*—Jaxson pulls back with his fingers wrapped around my waist, holding my gyrating hips in place.

"Damn." He pins me with his bright blue eyes that glow despite the growing darkness of my living room. "That's going to have to hold me until the next time we see each other."

"When do you think that will be?"

He shakes his head. "We have an away game this weekend and the coach promised to have us busy from seven to seven starting on Wednesday for the foreseeable future."

"And your curfew is at eight?" I frown.

"Exactly." He rubs his thumb over the frown lines on my brow. "Don't worry, baby. We'll figure it out."

I lean forward and rest my cheek against his chest. "I miss you already." The words slip out before I can think through their meaning.

He wraps his arms around me and rests his cheek against the top of my head. "I'm right here whenever you need me."

Chapter Seven
Jepson

When Jaxson comes home, I'm in my room. I promised myself I wouldn't ask him how the date went, wouldn't text Maryanne until tomorrow—not because I'm jealous, but because I'm weirdly not. I've never willingly shared anything with Jaxson unless it was my idea. That's the screwed-up part of my brain. I have no problem being part of a team, working together, give-and-take and all that shit—as long as it's my idea. Someone else tells me I have to do something and I rebel like the pain in the ass I am.

Why? I don't know.

Of course, I'm curious about how their date went.

Did she tell him she was not down with the arrangement I dropped in her lap this morning?

Is she going to ghost me tomorrow?

Did she ghost him tonight, and he's been driving around for hours?

Did they get along great and she invited him into her house?

To her bed?

I have a dozen questions, but I don't want to say or do something dickish, which I would have inevitably done had I been waiting on the couch for Jaxson to come home. The simple fact is, I don't want to fuck this up. I want Maryanne, but I don't want to take her from Jaxson to have her. We've never been really into the same woman before, so this is uncharted territory for us.

So I'm hiding in my room, watching TV and searching for self-help articles online. Somewhere out there is a book or podcast that will tell me in one-to-two concise sentences how to forgive myself for the past so I can stop being an asshole at large.

Tomorrow, I have breakfast plans with Rex. We went to dinner tonight and contemplated running up to Denver to have a drink with the ladies at the club, but again, my heart wasn't in it.

At least this time I know why—Maryanne Merry-weather.

I climb out of bed and walk down the hallway to Jaxson's room, knocking on his door. I hear his shower running and wonder why, but stomp that curiosity into the ground and open the door to yell from the threshold. "Hey man!"

"What's up?" Jaxson yells back at the same time he shuts off the water.

"Rex and I are meeting for breakfast tomorrow around eight. Then we were going to head to the Auto

Mall. He's got his eye on a new Tesla. Do you want to come?"

Jaxson walks out of his bathroom with a towel wrapped around his waist. My eyes quickly search his body for hickies, scratches, or any other telltale sign of sex. Finding none, I fixate on the scars lining his neck and the tattoos he got in college—ink that he got to draw people's eyes away from said reminders of the day he almost died.

Neither one of us likes to talk about it. He feels guilty because it was his puking blood in the car that distracted our mother, causing her to swing into oncoming traffic. I know this without him ever saying the words out loud. But that was an accident and considering he was hours from dying because of complications from acute pancreatitis, he's lucky he's alive today.

Until that moment, they were on their way home, not to the hospital, and if they had made it, he would have died sometime that night. No doubt in the doctor's mind.

But while he feels guilty about something he had no control over, I earned my guilt one hundred and ten percent. When Jaxson got sick in school, I took him to the bathroom and called our mother. Then I waited with him in the nurse's office, telling her where she could stick it when she suggested I go back to class.

Call it twin intuition, but I knew something was wrong.

When our mother showed up, I begged her to let me come with them, but she accused me of using my brother as an excuse to get out of school so I could dick around at home. She told me to go back to class to finish the day. I got so angry I lashed out, screaming how she babied Jaxson while treating me like an unwanted stepson. I called her every name a fourteen-year-old can think of, certain if I whined loud enough, I would get my way.

Those were the last words I spoke to my mother. Horrible things where I said I hated her and couldn't wait until the day I could move far away.

I'll never be able to take those words back.

Never be able to tell her how much I loved her and how she was the best mom a spoiled brat like me could ever have. I live with that regret every day. Mostly, I deal with it, but occasionally I get overrun with an uncontrollable rage fueled by self-loathing.

I never actively look to fight with Jaxson, but he makes it easy, always throwing himself in the way as if he thinks taking my shit is his penance when it's me who needs to atone for my sins.

"Yo! Earth to Jepson."

"Huh?" I glance up from the floor I've been unwittingly staring at.

He frowns. "I said, how the hell is Rex going to fit his big ass into a Tesla?"

I shake my head, shrugging off the memories and dark clouds that inevitably come when I think too much. "They're pretty roomy inside—lack of an engine and all that shit. Anyway, I have clown car music queued up on my phone, so it should be a good time, regardless."

He chuckles. "I'm in."

"Cool."

"Are you okay?"

I force a smile. "Yeah, I'm great. As always."

"Are you going to ask me about my date?" He raises his brow.

I shake my head again. "No. Although, I should mention that I actively avoided telling Rex about Maryanne tonight. Something tells me we should keep this between the three of us for now."

"Agreed."

I slap his door frame and wrap my fingers around the doorknob, preparing to leave. "Well, I'm going to go to bed. I'll see you in the morning."

"Goodnight, Jeps."

The next morning flies by, which I'm thankful for, considering I am far too inside my head for my comfort. I started the morning with a good morning text to Maryanne, relieved when she replied within minutes. Then around lunch, she let me know her day was spiraling out of control and she would let me know at four when and where I could pick her up.

To be honest, I've been waiting for her to cancel on me all day and am relieved she still sounds optimistic, if not frazzled.

At four o'clock, my phone rings.

"Hey beautiful," I plaster a smile on my face to make sure it comes through in my voice, but my gut twists in knots, as I suspect this is the inevitable cancellation. I've been waiting for it all day.

"Hey you. Today has kind of been a mess. I'm running late and I know you only have a very short amount of time, so would you be okay with picking me up at the office?"

Thank God she's not canceling on me.

"That's not a problem. What time?"

"Sometime between four thirty and five? I just got my employees out of here and I have a few things to tie up before I can sign off for the day."

"I will hop in the car now and we'll play it by ear. Does that sound good?"

"Yes, and thank you so much for being understanding, Jepson."

"Hey, I'm happy to spend some time with you. Plus, our schedules are pretty crazy, so I can sympathize."

"Great. See you soon, handsome." She hangs up and I blow out a breath of relief.

Forty-five minutes later, I roll up in front of her business. I might carry myself like a cocky, egotistical asshole, but I am filled with insecurities like everyone else. Especially when confronted by someone who I know is too good for me.

Maryanne is definitely too good for someone like me.

An electronic bell dings overhead as I enter the building.

"Hey you," Maryanne says from the depths of her office, reminding me of our initial meeting yesterday.

I stop at the threshold of her office. On her desk are a

flurry of paperwork, two empty paper coffee cups, a half-eaten sandwich and a bouquet of pink and white roses. "Did my brother bring you those flowers yesterday?"

She glances up from her computer. "Yeah, he did."

"Beautiful." I walk into her office and circle her desk, leaning forward and planting a chaste kiss against her cheek. "How are you doing, sweetheart?"

"I'm good," she sighs. "I'm so sorry things got a little crazy today."

I shake my head. "You never have to apologize to me for being busy. Trust me, we are well aware of not being in control of our schedules or our free time." Why do I keep including Jaxson in the conversation?

"I have to send this email. So if you give me like five minutes, I can put everything down and we can go."

"Take all the time you need." I take a step back and motion to her computer. "Is it confidential?"

"The email? No. Just a list of things I need to send out to my team so they can organize themselves instead of me spending half my day dictating to them what they need to be doing."

I slide behind her chair and put my hands on her shoulders, rubbing softly at first and using my thumb to put pressure against the knots in her neck.

"Oh," she moans. "That's so good."

Encouraged, I massage a little harder as she types out the last of her email. As soon as she hits send, I pull the pencil holding her hair up in some makeshift bun, letting her long locks loose to fall around her shoulder.

"I love your hair," I murmur as I run her strands through my fingers before kissing the top of her head.

"I'm ready to get out of here." She tilts her head back to look up at me.

Goddamn, her lips are so fucking plump and kissable. "Are you sure?"

"Yes, I have everything at the perfect stopping point for me to pick up tomorrow. Are we going somewhere that I need to change clothes for or can I go like this?" She motions to her jeans and silky blouse.

"You can go like that." I pull her chair back from the desk and swing her around to face me, placing my hands on the armrest so that I'm hovering over her. I'm tempted to kiss her now, but I don't want to scare her off.

She licks her lips and smiles, not backing down one bit from me. "Where are we going?"

"I have a surprise for you." I grin, offering her my hand.

She tosses her sandwich and coffee cups into the trash, grabs her purse, and then takes my hand.

We walk outside and she gasps as I hit the unlock on my car. "Is this yours?"

"Maybe. Rex wanted to test drive Teslas today, and they had this sitting on the lot as a trade-in. I haven't decided if I'm going to keep it or not." I walk her to the passenger side of the convertible.

"Well, it's beautiful." She bites her lip and looks back at me as I open the door. "What is it?"

I chuckle. "Not much of a car aficionado, huh?"

"No, not really."

"Yeah, me neither. This is a Jaguar F-Type."

"Is it fast?" Her eyes sparkle as she sits down in the passenger seat.

I recognize that look. "Do you want to drive it?"

"Really?"

I offer her my hand, pull her to her feet and escort her from the passenger to the driver's side. Handing her the keys, I lean in and place a kiss against her neck. "Don't get a ticket."

She pulls her hair up in a messy clip as I step around to the passenger side. "I'm so nervous. I've never driven a car this fancy before. Look! It has paddle shifters."

I chuckle but say nothing. Her excitement is infectious and my heart expands with childlike glee.

"Where should we go?" she says as she hits the button to start the car. It's a V8 and has a low rumble when it idles.

"Well, I had planned to take you somewhere we could have a picnic dinner, but if you really want to open her up, we're going to have to get on the freeway."

"Which park were you thinking of having a picnic at?"

"Pickers Point. I heard the sunsets are amazing from there and it's not that far away."

She giggles, putting the car in reverse and backing out of the parking space with overzealous care. "You know that's a high school make-out spot, right?"

I shake my head. "I didn't go to high school here, and I don't date high school girls. Did you go up there a lot in high school?"

She giggles again and rolls her eyes. "No, boys didn't invite me to places like that."

"Then how do you know it's a make-out city?"

"Rumor mill about this person or that person doing this or that."

"I was thinking we'd have a picnic, but if this or that comes up, I'm not opposed."

She navigates a series of turns and we appear to be heading south. "I should tell you something before we get too far away from my car."

"Okay?" I don't like her ominous tone. What bad news could she have for me already?

"I don't... I think it's best if we don't have sex until we know exactly how this is going to play out between the three of us."

I kind of expected this, so I nod and say nothing.

She glances at me quickly, then puts her eyes back on the road. "Are you mad?"

Shaking my head, I turn to look at her. "No, but what happens if you decide after a couple of dates that you like both of us?"

Rolling to a stop at the light, she hits the turn signal to head to the interstate. "I've been thinking about that a lot and honestly, I don't know. I don't know what to do."

I slide my hand on top of her thigh and squeeze right above her knee. "You are overthinking this, Maryanne. Jaxson and I are good. We spent all morning together, and I even talked to him last night when he got home from your date."

"You did?" she squeaks.

"Yeah, and I didn't ask him one question about your night together. I didn't want to make him uncomfortable, and I didn't want to fill my head with preconceived notions coming into tonight. All I want is to get to know you, and yes, I desperately want to touch you, but I can wait until you're ready—if that's what you need."

She slides her hand on top of mine and squeezes my fingers. "Thank you. You're right, I'm overthinking this, but how often does something like this work? Dating two guys is one thing. Two brothers, significantly different. Two identical twins living in the same house, playing on the same team—I mean, that has to be super rare. Like one in a billion."

"I would think you'd be used to having men fight for your attention. Maybe not twin brothers, but multiple men, definitely."

She scoffs. "Not likely."

"Maryanne, I don't think you realize how stunning you are. Beautiful, inside and out, but you also have this untapped sex appeal that I recognized from across the room the day we met."

Sliding her eyes my way momentarily, she takes a left to merge onto I-25 southbound. "How fast am I allowed to go?"

"As fast as you want, gorgeous." It's rush hour, and while the interstate isn't packed, there are enough cars that she only gets to go fast in short spurts, but it's enough to have her giggling like a maniac as the wind blows through our hair. Two miles up the road, she takes the exit, drives over the overpass, and merges back onto the interstate to head north toward downtown. The entire trip takes less than fifteen minutes before we're driving down inner city streets toward Picker's Point.

"This is a fun car. Why wouldn't you keep it?"

"For all the money we make, Jaxson and I are quite frugal. Call it a side effect of growing up poor, but neither of us splurges on unnecessary things. Like the BMW he drives, he bought it used and has had it for three years."

"Is that why you guys share a place? To save money?"

"No, I don't know that we ever thought about doing it any other way. Honestly, I don't know why he hangs around me sometimes."

"You're his brother. He loves you."

I shrug. "Maybe."

Maryanne drives us past the park entrance, stopping at a fork in the road. "Do you want to drive to the top?"

"Is that where everyone is making out?" I waggle my brows and give her a playful grin.

She shakes her head and tries not to smile. "The sun is still up, so I doubt anybody's making out right now, but I believe there are picnic tables up there."

"Let's do it."

The road winds up a miniature mountain located smack dab in the middle of Spring City—a thousand feet of elevation gained in the short drive. She parks the car in a nearly empty parking lot, and I grab two bags of groceries out of the trunk.

"How many people are we feeding?" Maryanne giggles.

I shrug. "I wasn't sure what you would be in the

mood for, so I got us a bit of everything."

"Do you have dietary restrictions like your brother?"

"No. I have an ironclad stomach."

"Does it bother you if I mention your brother?"

"No." We sit at a picnic table at the edge of the property overlooking a cliff. I pull out a dozen containers from the deli, and then offer her a plastic-wrapped silverware set. "Next time I'll take you somewhere fancy."

She shakes her head with a huge smile on her face. "This is one hundred percent my speed."

"Do you mind sharing food out of the same container? I figured we could dig in, family style."

"I love it." We eat in silence for a few minutes, sampling fresh salads, slaw, and who knows what else. I told the deli to give me a smattering of everything they had, which included roasted and fried chicken.

"Can I ask you a question?" Maryanne says between bites.

"Anything." I crack open a flavored seltzer water and hand it to her.

"The gentlemen's clubs—what's the attraction? I mean, you're a good-looking guy, college educated, and you have an amazing job I assume pays very well—"

"Do you know any exotic dancers?" I break in to stop her rambling.

She blushes and shakes her head. "No, I guess I don't. Do I sound judgy? I don't mean to be, but I'm curious about what's going on in a person's mind. What's their motivation behind the worlds they create for themselves?"

Chapter Eight
Maryanne

"I like gentlemen's clubs because you know exactly what you're going to get there. For instance, the people there play mind games, but everybody knows and expects it. Does that make any sense?"

"Kind of."

"The dancers know why they're there and what they're trying to sell. The patrons also know why they're there and what they're trying to buy. Anyone who doesn't understand the rules of the establishment learns quickly. Also, I find the people fascinating."

"Have you dated a lot of dancers?"

He shakes his head. "I have never dated one dancer in Colorado. I did date a girl in college who danced on the weekends to pay for school. She was my introduction into that world."

"So it's not about sex for you?"

"Have you ever been to a strip club?"

"No." I blush again. Damn, I didn't mean to come across as such a judgmental bitch. Am I?

"Do you want to?" He grins. "I think you'd find it pretty interesting, especially if you're into people-watching. Obviously, the dancers are beautiful, and some are talented, and yes, all are nearly nude, but the patrons are even more interesting. The interaction between the dancers and the customers is a study in non-verbal communication."

"You speak about it with reverence, as if you respect the dancers."

"I do, mostly."

"So then, how did you get kicked out of a couple of them?"

He sighs. "I'm sure it's not a stretch of the imagination that I can be a true asshole from time to time. Occasionally, my mouth runs before my brain can think through what's coming out."

I smile. "At least you know that about yourself."

He snorts. "Yeah, it's controlling it that's the problem."

"Where do you think that stems from?" Good god, my inner psychologist is really coming out right now.

He narrows his eyes. "If you're going to psychoanalyze me, I'm going to need you to sit in my lap so I have an emotional support animal to hold on to."

"Are you calling me an animal?" I giggle.

He waggles his eyebrows again. He's always flirting, even when I don't think he means to be. "I'm saying I want to snuggle you."

I bite my lip and look at the food scattered across the table. "Can I feed you cake at the same time?"

Something akin to a growl comes from his throat. "Yes."

I get up from my side of the table and walk over to sit next to him. He changes his position to straddle the bench with one leg on either side and pulls me between his splayed legs, draping my knees over his thick thigh. Once again, he pulls my hair free of the soft scrunchie and finger combs my tangled locks. He kisses my temple, and then my cheek, before nipping my earlobe between his teeth.

An involuntary shiver courses through my limbs, and my breath hitches with a soft moan as I relax into his embrace.

"So you used to be a therapist?" he says as I lean against his chest and he plays with my hair.

"Did Jaxson tell you that?"

"No, I saw your diploma on your office wall."

"Oh, I forgot about that. Sorry, I'm sure I'm killing in the mood with all of my psychobabble."

"I could easily prove to you that you have not killed the mood, but I'm trying to be a gentleman." His voice rumbles in his chest, reverberating against my cheek.

I pull back to look him in the eye, my gaze sliding down his body to look at the bulge in his slacks. "Oh my."

"Yeah."

"You're going to make it hard to say no, aren't you?"

"I'm not going to make it easy," he answers honestly.

"I guess it's lucky we're in a public place then." I arch my brow.

"Something tells me all of our dates are going to be public for the foreseeable future." He winks.

"I could go for semi-private."

He shakes his head. "Fuck, Maryanne, you are something special."

"How long until you have to take me back to my car?"

He glances at his watch. "I have thirty minutes before we have to get going."

Another two couples come into the picnic area and set up for the sunset. I knew that was going to happen and feel like this is an excellent time for us to find someplace a little more private. "Maybe you should take me back now, so we can have some time alone before you have to go?"

Jepson cups my jaw with his large hand and leans forward, pressing his lips to mine. I close my eyes, prepared to melt into him, but he ends the kiss quickly by sucking my lower lip into his mouth and letting it go with a pop. "Let's go. The way I want to kiss you is not fitting for teenage eyes."

We pack up and are driving down the road in minutes, Jepson behind the wheel this time, his hand resting high on my thigh. I'll admit, after my make-out session with Jaxson last night, I opted for pants today because I was certain Jepson would be handsier than his twin.

Honestly, he's been more of a gentleman than I was expecting, even though every look he throws my way lets me know he wants to devour every inch of me. He doesn't hide it.

The gods must want me to have this and him because we hit nothing but green lights on our way back to my office. As soon as I unlock the door, Jepson has me in his arms, his hands under my ass, pulling me up around his waist. He carries me to my desk, his mouth on my neck, lips trailing kisses down my collarbone. His movements are frantic as he pulls my blouse loose from my jeans, and before I know it, I'm allowing him to slide the loose silk over my head.

"Wait," I see breathlessly. "What are you doing?"

"Taking our shirts off."

"We can't."

"Sweet Maryanne, we don't have time for sex. But I want to feel your skin against mine." He unbuttons his shirt and slides it off of his broad shoulders. Where last night I felt the chiseled muscle on Jaxson through his shirt, tonight Jepson is showing me what a well-defined athlete's body looks like.

"Oh wow," I murmur, running my fingers over his eight-pack.

He grins. "I'm glad you like it."

Then he sits in one of my armless chairs and pulls me into his lap. His fabric-clad erection hits my denim-covered pussy as he pulls me tight against him. His hands slide over my breast, his fingers deftly finding my nipples while his mouth covers mine, his tongue dancing along my lips. Whereas Jaxson was tempered and methodical in his touch, Jepson is raw need—touching me everywhere at the same time. He shifts his hips, dry-humping me with the kind of desperation that makes me want to shed my clothes and spread wide for him.

"Fuck, I want to taste you so bad."

I whimper because I want that too.

He unhooks my bra—his lips, teeth, and tongue toying with my nipples before I realize I've been exposed. I can't stop him now, arching into his hands, completely lost to his commanding touch—all temperance and reason gone. If he makes a move for the buttons of my jeans, I don't think I'm going to be able to stop him.

"Tell me something." Jepson looks up at me from between my breasts, his hands kneading and pushing them together so that he can suck each nipple into his mouth without moving his head.

"What?"

"Did you and Jaxson make out last night?"

I suck in my breath and nod slowly.

"And after he left, were you so turned on that you had to get yourself off?"

I bite my lip. "Yes."

"I'm pretty sure he got himself off as soon as he got home, too, which is exactly what I'm going to do when I get home tonight. But, sweet Maryanne, if you'd let me, I'll get you off before I go without ever taking off your pants."

That has to be the best sales pitch I've ever heard. "How are you going to do that?"

He lifts two fingers to my mouth, sliding them past my lips to suck on them, a tinge of guilt infusing my skin as I realize that I'm about to go much farther with Jepson than with Jaxson last night. How can I treat them equally when they approach me so differently?

Jepson pops the buttons on my jeans and slides the zipper down. Then he pulls his fingers out of my mouth, sliding them down my belly and inside my panties. I don't stop him. Instead, I have my eyes glued to his as he slides his fingers over my clit, circling slowly.

I gasped, involuntarily bucking my hips forward.

He grins. "That's my sweet girl, but you've got to fuck my fingers," he says at the same time he slides them inside of me. It's a tight fit with my jeans on, and I lift so they sag a bit on my hips.

He growls his approval, curving his hand and pumping his fingers to plunge deeper inside of me. As his thumb circles my clit, Jepson breaks eye contact and latches onto my nipple, scraping the tender flesh with his teeth.

It takes nothing for me to lose myself to him, riding his hand as he quickly brings me to the edge of release.

I grip his shoulders, digging my fingernails into the thick wall of muscle around his neck. "Oh god, oh my god, Jepson, oh my god." I shatter into a million pieces, his hand pumping hard and fast against my pussy.

"Fuck—" he barks "—you are so fucking sexy."

Unable to form words, I have my head thrown back as my cunt grips his fingers tight, riding out my climax.

I bring my head down at the same time he pulls his fingers out of me, lifting them to his mouth and sucking them clean. "Next time, I'm doing that with my mouth."

"Oh wow," I say, because what else can I say? Two and a half hours with Jepson and I've already broken the only rule I threw out there as part of this whole arrangement.

No sex.

He pulls me down onto his lap and kisses me deeply, his tongue once again tangling with mine. "I knew you would taste as sweet as you look."

"You are dangerous to be around."

"Why?"

"I don't think I'm going to be able to tell you no."

Jepson wraps his arms around me lovingly, pulling me into a tender hug. "If you really wanted to say no, you would. It's my job to make you think hard about it."

It's been six weeks of texts, phone calls, and stolen moments. Jaxson and Jepson have been working hard from sun up to sun down, yet they always find time to make me feel special, reminding me daily they are thinking of me. At least once a week Jaxson swings by my place on his way home from practice. We make out in fevered haste, and even though I've suggested we take it to the bedroom, he's the one pumping the brakes because he doesn't want our first time to be rushed. As he so poetically says, "The first time I feel you wrapped around me, I want to be able to savor it."

That hasn't stopped him from getting me off with his fingers and mouth multiple times.

Jepson has also swung by my place on his way home. The last couple of times he's laid me out on my coffee table and eaten my pussy with such toe-curling skill, I've taken to wearing skirts when greeting him. He's much more carnal than Jaxson, but he also wants to wait on sex until we have time to enjoy it. As he said, fifteen minutes isn't going to work for him.

What's weirder than having two men hold off on sex? Neither of them has let me reciprocate, even though I've tried. To say I'm frustrated would be an understatement, but at least I've been getting off. I can't imagine how on edge they are right now.

I'm laying in bed contemplating these real-world problems when my phone beeps with a group text—the first one we've shared between the three of us.

> Jepson: Sweet, tasty, Maryanne. Jaxson and I were talking about your upcoming birthday. Do you have plans?

> London wants to take me to lunch, but otherwise no.

> Jaxson: We'd like to do something for you. Together.

I sit up and stare at my phone.

Together?

I'll admit, I've fantasized about spending time with both of them, although I'm unsure how that would work.

I mean, I can imagine how two men share one woman—but brothers? That can't be what they mean by together.

> What did you have in mind?

> Jaxson: Well, since we're still on lockdown, we'd figure you could come over to our place and have dinner, cake, and a movie.

> Jepson: Yeah, and as soon as our curfew is lifted we'll take you out dancing or something. Rumor is curfew will be lifted soon.

> When?

> Jaxson: Tomorrow night. We fly out Saturday to Seattle.

> Are you sure about this—the three of us hanging out together?

> Jepson: Yeah, we've talked at length about it, and we're both cool.

> Then I'd love to spend my birthday with you.

> Jaxson: Fantastic. Eight pm, our place.

The group text dies, but both of them send me individual texts wishing me sweet dreams before they sign off for the night. Excitement fills my belly, and any tiredness I felt from my busy workday dissipates. I think about calling London, but ever since she and Deacon made their relationship real, she's been impossible to get a hold of. He pretty much moved her into his place the next day.

Still, I need someone to talk to.

Hey, are you available to chat?

My phone rings instantly. "Hey, you. Everything okay?"

"Yeah. Am I bothering you?"

"Nope. Just lounging here waiting for Deacon to get home."

I look at the time again. "It's late. He's not home yet?"

"No. I guess they are having a management meeting about the team. They are leading the league at six and one, but I guess cracks are forming in team cohesion."

"Well, they have been on lockdown with a ridiculous curfew for over a month."

My outburst is met with silence.

"How do you know about the curfew?" I can hear the smile on her lips and realize I just outed myself. I told her I'd been asked out by two guys, and I told her I was dating both, but I carefully omitted their names and team affiliation.

"I..."

"Holy shit, Maryanne. Are you dating football players?"

"Oh god. Do you think Deidre will fire me?"

She chuckles. "I think I would avoid having the team find out until you decide where it is going."

"You have to promise you won't tell Deacon." I plead.

She sighs. "Oh, I won't be the one to tell Deacon. Trust me. He's stressed enough without thinking he's going to have to smack around a couple of his players for mistreating my best friend. So, where is this going?"

"Uh, right now it's heading toward a double date for my birthday this Friday."

"Double date? How are they going to pull that off with their curfew?"

"By having me come to their place so they're not out after hours."

"Oh, the plot thickens. So, they not only know about each other, but they're roommates?" she squeaks, and I can imagine her rubbing her palms together as she unwraps my devious plans.

There are no devious plans.

"Yeah."

"Oh, come on Maryanne. You have to tell me who it is."

"Are you sure you want to know? You'll have to make eye contact with them and pretend like you don't know."

"Oh, good point." She whistles under her breath. "Yeah, I want to know."

I sigh. "Jepson and Jaxson Masters."

Absolute silence.

"Hello?"

"The twins?" London giggles so hard, she snorts. "Really, Maryanne? My sweet, innocent best friend is dating identical twins?"

"So far, we've only had one date each. Otherwise, it's been twenty-minute make-out sessions and that's it."

"Wow. And I thought Deacon and my situation was scandalous."

"What am I going to do?" I whine, even though I already know what I'm going to do. I'm showing up at their house wearing a fun flirty dress, prepared for anything. I'll let them set the pace, considering we'll be in their home, but I'm not going to wimp out.

At least, that's the plan.

"You like them, so I guess you're having dinner at their place tomorrow night."

"And when one leans in to kiss me?"

"You kiss him back."

"What if one invites me up to his room?"

"Yeesh. I don't know about that one. I guess it would depend on what's going on at that moment. Are both aware one is moving you to the bedroom? Are they planning on taking turns with you? Are you hopping from one room to the other?" She giggles again. "Oh my god, I can't believe I'm talking about something like this with you, of all people. It's always the quiet ones... I am so glad we're having lunch on Saturday."

"You're not going to be able to look me in the eye the next time you see me."

"You know I love you more than anything. You are my best friend and I'm not judging you in any way. As long as you are happy, that's all I care about."

"Things are still up in the air, but I am having fun right now."

"And there's nothing wrong with that."

Chapter Nine
Jaxson

After a month of cold showers, Jepson threw down the gauntlet this morning, telling me what we have to do regarding Maryanne.

"We'll invite her over for dinner. That way we're not breaking curfew, and we're not rushing through a date."

"And then what?"

Jepson shrugs. "We see how it goes. You talk to her daily and see her when you can. You've held her, touched her, kissed her—and so have I. I assume you haven't fucked, but I'm willing to bet you've gotten her off as often as possible—"

"Jesus, man." I slide my hand down my face. We haven't talked about our individual time with Maryanne, but knowing her, if one of us is doing it, both of us are. Otherwise, she'd feel guilty about it. I have no doubt in my mind anything I've done with her, Jepson did first. That's his speed, zero to ninety in two point eight seconds.

"What? We've talked about all this shit before with other women, and yes, Maryanne is special, but I'm tired of pussyfooting around here. I know what I want, and I know what she wants, and I'm pretty sure I know what you want, and I don't think we're going to be able to move forward unless we figure out a way to share her."

I scoff. "You've never shared anything with me in your life."

"Not true. We shared a womb for over eight months and many other things growing up to include pets, cars, and friends. Then there was Christie Snow in middle school. We took turns playing doctor with her in the tree-house, remember?" He waggles his brows.

"Geez, I forgot about her." Of course, Christie Snow was playing doctor with a lot of boys back then, and later girls too.

"And there were several girls in high school and college we both dated—"

"Not at the same time," I interject.

"And a couple drunk nights in college with a few sorority sisters," he continues.

"Maryanne is not a sorority sister and we're not in college anymore."

Jepson pinches the bridge of his nose and sighs. "I'm falling in love with her, Jaxs, and I'm pretty sure you are, too. I'd rather share her with you than lose her. Can you say differently?"

There it is. Leave it to Jepson to lay it out plainly. "No, but how is this going to work?"

He shrugs again. "Follow my lead and it will all work out like it is supposed to."

That was yesterday morning, and now we're wrapping up the end of our Friday, praying that the team-wide curfew lifts soon. Tension is growing, and after our loss last week, everyone seems a bit more on edge.

"You guys want to hang out tonight?" Rex says between us.

I glance at Jepson and then down at my shoes.

"Can't tonight," Jepson says. "I thought you'd have a visitor tonight, anyway. What's her name again?"

Rex has been loosely seeing this woman for a few months, but their relationship seems to be strictly bedroom bound.

"I think she's dating someone. I haven't heard from her much lately." Rex frowns.

"Bummer." Jepson slaps his shoulder.

"What do you two have going on tonight?"

"Birthday celebration with a close friend." I blurt out.

"How are you going to pull that off with curfew?" Rex raises his brow.

"She's coming over to our house." Jepson glances at me with a subtle shake of his head.

Rex narrows his eyes, his head swiveling comically to look at both of us. "I don't want to know, do I?"

"You're one of our best friends. When there is something to tell you, we will," Jepson says casually, sliding his hands into his pockets before looking at me. "You ready?"

"Yeah." I follow my brother out of the locker room and down the corridor to the garage.

He chuckles. "What the hell is wrong with you?"

"I don't know." I shrug. "This is weird."

"It's only weird if you make it weird, and I'm telling you right now, Jaxson, Maryanne is going to feed off your nervous energy, so knock it off."

I take a deep breath and let it out slowly, using the drive home to clear my head. We have a caterer arriving at seven-thirty to set up, and I ordered flowers to be delivered at seven-thirty and eight. When we get home, the caterer and florist are both waiting in our driveway, so I run up and take a shower while Jepson deals with them. By the time I come down, the caterers are gone and the kitchen smells like an Italian restaurant. There are bouquets and balloons all over the place, as well as champagne sitting in an ice bucket next to three glasses and a platter of chocolate-covered strawberries with a tiny birthday cake and one solitary candle.

Neither Jepson nor I like champagne.

"I think you went overboard on the flowers." Jepson chuckles as he pulls off his shirt.

"Champagne?"

He shrugs. "It's appropriate."

"Think she'll like it?"

"Yeah, I do." He runs up the stairs. "Speaking of which, she texted and is on her way. I opened the garage door for her to pull in. You'll hear her when she drives up."

"Got it."

Five minutes later, I'm opening the door as Maryanne rolls to a stop and shuts off her engine. My hand is on her door before she has a chance to unfasten her seatbelt, and I have her in my arms, my lips pressed to hers before she can yelp hello.

Maryanne throws her arms around my neck, sinking into my chest.

"Welcome home," I say without thinking twice about the words. They feel right. Having her here is one hundred percent the right move.

Dammit, Jepson was right, again.

She smiles at me. "I missed you, too."

"Are you hungry? I think Jepson ordered an entire restaurant." I take her hand and escort her into the house, closing the garage door behind us.

"It smells amaz—"

I turn to see what stopped her words. Her eyes bounce around the living room and kitchen, taking in all the flowers and balloons and everything else. "Is this all for me?"

"Of course."

Tears spring to her eyes. "Really?"

"Baby." I pull her into my arms. "Who else would they be for?"

She wraps her arms around my waist and shakes her head. "I was so nervous and excited about coming here tonight, but I didn't expect all of this."

"You should never accept anything less." I kiss the top of her head, her temple, and then claim her lips when she tilts her face up to mine. I'm on the verge of lifting her into my arms and carrying her into the living room when Jepson chuckles from the stairway.

"Damn, man. Did you even offer her a drink yet?"

"Dammit," I grumble and pull back an inch. "What would you like to drink?"

She slides her hands down my arms and takes a step back. "I could go for a mixed drink. Vodka and anything."

Jepson is beside us in an instant, sliding his hand over the small of her back and leaning down to plant a kiss on her neck even though she is still technically in my arms. "You look beautiful, sweetheart."

Maryanne smiles at him. "Thank you."

"Are you hungry?" Jepson takes her hand and guides her to the table where three place settings are set. He pulls out the chair at the head of our smaller six-person table where she takes her seat.

"What are we having?"

"You mentioned loving Luigi's chicken piccata, so I had it brought in along with a smattering of appetizers."

"I did? It's true, I love it, but I don't remember us talking about it."

I walk up with her drink called a Godmother. It's vodka and amaretto, but I added a splash of seltzer to dilute it. As I set the glass down, I hear Jepson whisper loudly, "I might have been distracting you when you told me about your favorite foods."

Maryanne blushes, her eyes growing wide. "Oh."

"Want me to grab the plates?" I mutter, completely unsure of what to do while Jepson flirts with my woman.

Our woman, but also mine.

"Nah, man. I got it. Go ahead and take a seat." Jepson smacks me lightly on the shoulder and then walks away casually, leaving me to choose between sitting on Maryanne's right or left.

"What's this?" She lifts the drink to her nose and sniffs.

"Vodka and amaretto. If you don't like it, I'll make you something else." I sit to her right, my left hand immediately finding its way to her thigh.

She sips her drink and hums her pleasure. "Mmmm. Yummy."

Jepson walks in with two plates, hers and mine. "Little known fact about Jaxson. He took a bartending class in college, hence why we have an amazing bar and he's always on drink duty."

Maryanne swings her surprise my way. "Really? But you don't drink."

I grin and give a little shrug of my shoulders. "I drink a little, but you can imagine how popular the sober football player is at college parties. I needed a way to stay relevant while not getting shit-faced, outside of being the designated driver."

Jepson walks in with two more plates, his and the smattering of appetizers he alluded to. "He can make anything, even fancy drinks, and he's damn good at it."

I look at him and wonder why he's pumping me up and when the hammer is going to fall. Is he setting me up so that he can knock me down later? His attitude about this entire situation has me completely off-kilter.

"Really? What's your favorite drink to make?" She keeps the conversation moving.

"It's not necessarily a specific drink, it's more about

taking normal drinks and shaking them up a bit with something different or special."

"For example?" She picks up her fork after Jepson takes his seat to her left.

"Like making a lemon drop martini, and then adding lavender-infused liqueur to it. It gives it a slightly different flavor without getting overly complicated."

"It's all about variety and understanding what will work well together," Jepson adds, his hidden meaning landing with the subtlety of a boulder.

Maryanne looks down at her plate, twirling the tines of her fork in the lemony sauce. "Something tells me I'm gonna learn more from you dishing on your brother than I will from asking you questions directly."

"What else would you like to know, baby?" I take a bite of my roasted chicken with marsala sauce. "Do you want to know about the time Jepson broke his arm trying to parachute off the top of our treehouse?"

Jepson rolls his eyes. "I was ten years old, and I'm pretty sure you told me if I believed hard enough I could do anything."

"I didn't mean defy the laws of gravity."

Maryanne giggles. "I've barely experienced the two of you together. It's nice."

She takes a bite of her dinner and moans softly. "You have to try this, it is so good." She offers me a bite, and then cuts up a second piece, offering it to Jepson.

I make eye contact with my brother and smile. This feels so normal that my anxiety about this evening slowly melts away as we descend into stories from our childhood, most of which are embarrassing for both of us.

Maryanne devours about half her plate and then sets her fork down, sipping the last of her drink.

"Do you want another one? Or maybe some champagne?" I ask.

"Champagne?"

"Well, this is a celebration—strawberries and champagne go well together."

"I love chocolate-covered strawberries," Maryanne coos.

Jepson stands and grabs her plate before leaning forward and kissing her neck. "I know, sweetheart."

I grab my plate and the leftover appetizers and follow him into the kitchen, telling her to remain seated. I look into my brother's bright blue eyes shining with unfettered happiness. "This is going well," I say low under my breath.

He nods, "Keep following my lead."

I grab champagne flutes and the bottle, popping the cork and pouring three glasses—ours filled significantly less than hers.

Jepson follows with a plate of strawberries and a small tiramisu cake. He lights the lone candle and sets it in front of her. "Happy birthday, sweetheart."

I lean forward and tilt her face up to mine, kissing her chastely on the lips. "We'll save you from our singing."

She smiles and swings her eyes to Jepson who lovingly brushes a piece of hair behind her ear. "Make a wish."

To my surprise, she grabs our hands—the three of us joined in a Maryanne-centric chain—and then leans forward to blow out her candle. She sits still with her eyes closed for several seconds. "This is the nicest birthday celebration I've had in a long time. Thank you both."

"It's not over yet." Jepson brings her hand up to his lips before letting go and taking the seat beside her.

"What movie are we watching?" she asks as I continue to stand next to her and play with her hair while Jepson lifts a chocolate covered strawberry to her mouth. Watching her wrap her lips around the plump berry while she stares into Jepson's eyes is arousing versus uncomfortable, as I suspected it would be. I wouldn't think watching my brother take control of the situation while seducing Maryanne would be a turn-on, but it is. I've seen him be every way with women. A cocky asshole —which works more often than not—or charmingly sweet like he is now. I'm glad he's being nice—otherwise, we'd have a problem.

A drop of strawberry juice dribbles down her chin and Jepson leans forward, licking it up and then kissing her with a lot more passion than he's shown thus far. Maryanne moans into his mouth, her right hand reaching out to grab my thigh—either to make sure I'm here or to include me. I'm assuming the latter.

"We rented that rom-com you were talking about last week. As soon as you're ready, we'll cuddle up on the couch and push play," Jepson murmurs against her lips before looking up at me. "Why don't you give Maryanne a tour of the house, and I'll rearrange the sofa for the movie?"

I nod, waiting until he stands and clears the cake from the table. Interlacing my fingers with hers, I pull her to her stunned feet. "Did his kiss make you dizzy?"

She smiles with a dazed expression on her face. "I feel like I'm in a dream."

"Which part, baby?" I guide her around the table and to the stairs, descending to the walkout basement where we house our gym, office, and arcade. I figure I'll leave the bedrooms for last to avoid temptation.

"All of it. Being pampered and thoroughly cared for by not just one, but two hot guys—it's every girl's fantasy."

"Is it?" I chuckle.

"Well, maybe not every girl, but being here with both of you feels a lot more comfortable than I thought it would."

"I agree. I was nervous about tonight too."

"And Jepson?"

"Jepson always plays cool and confident, regardless of how he's feeling on the inside."

Maryanne stops me at the bottom of the stairs and slips her fingers over my belt buckle, pulling me to her. "I care about both of you and don't want to lose either one of you. If you make me choose, I don't know what I'm going to do."

I cup her face in my hands and stare into her big brown eyes. "We're not going to make you choose. I don't know what tonight or the future looks like, but neither of us expects you to choose."

"How will this work?" She licks her lips.

Shaking my head, I swipe my thumb over her bottom lip. "I honestly don't know. I guess we do what feels good and don't worry about what's going on outside these walls when we're doing it."

"I want you, Jaxson. But I want Jepson too."

"I'm okay with that." I kiss her softly, but she's having none of it. She tightens her hands in my waistband, pulling our bodies flush as she lifts onto her tiptoes, trying to control our kiss. I slide my hands under her ass and pull her into my arms, pressing her back against the wall as she wraps her legs around my waist.

Maryanne is an addiction I don't think I'll ever shake. Her touch is intoxicating, her lips enticing, but I covet her heart most of all. She's perfect for me—funny, sweet, gentle, and passionate. It's been hell denying myself the pleasure she's been desperate to give me, but I know that once I feel her lips wrapped around me, I won't be able to stop, and team-imposed curfews and organization rules will mean nothing. I'm willing to bet Jepson has been having the same internal battle, only with a lot more anger. The fact he hasn't lashed out lately is all the more impressive considering I know how on edge I've been, and that's with a new starting position on the team—one that he seems genuinely excited for me to have.

I slide my hand under her skirt, my fingertips brushing along lace and silk. "I want you. Please don't deny me any longer." Maryanne pants and reaches between us to cup me through my slacks.

I groan, seconds away from undoing my pants and taking her right now against this wall.

"The movie is cued up and ready to go," Jepson calls from the top of the stairs.

"Be right there!" I call back, resting my forehead against hers. "I won't deny you again. You set the pace, baby, and we'll take care of whatever you want and need."

Chapter Ten
Maryanne

Jaxson sets me down and places a kiss on my forehead. "Let's go upstairs."

As we ascend the stairs, I make a decision. I'm going to set the pace all right, and claim my men who I know care for me as much as I care for them. I'm pretty sure I'm in love with them, and I have no idea how to deal with this knowledge because I've never been in love before.

Of course, I'd have to fall in love with two men my first time.

Walking into their house and seeing the flowers, balloons, and fancy foods, I saw men who figured out how to give me the world while having no time for themselves. Their ingenuity and thoughtfulness mean more to me than any gift.

I walk into the living room where their couch looks more like a double-sized chaise lounge; the backs reclined at a forty-five-degree angle. Jepson has all the windows darkened and the lights down low, his shoes off and his body stretched out on the far end of the couch.

"You can turn your couch into a bed?" I giggle as I pull off my heels and crawl onto the sofa into his waiting arms.

"We can turn this couch into anything you want. It's completely modular and adjustable."

"Fancy," I say, swinging my leg over his hips to straddle his lap. His eyes flash with heated surprise as I lean down and claim his mouth, kissing him with all the desire coursing through my veins. Jaxson got me started downstairs, and I refuse to tiptoe into our inevitable nakedness this evening. Jepson doesn't freeze for a second, one hand sliding up my thigh under my skirt, the other slipping into my hair, fisting a handful as he kisses me with as much need as I feel. "Take off your shirt."

He sits up and pulls off his shirt without hesitation, his body a glorious work of art.

I glance over my shoulder to find Jaxson missing from the room. "Jaxson?"

He pops his head out of the kitchen. "Yeah, baby?"

"Come here, please."

He tosses the dish towel in his hand onto a chair and kicks off his shoes as he approaches.

I lift my arms above my head. "Will you pull my dress off me?"

His eyes flicker to Jepson and then back to mine. Leaning down, he lowers the zipper that runs down the back of my dress while pressing kisses to my neck and shoulder. Then he takes the fabric gathered around my waist by Jepson and pulls it over my head. I'm wearing black and maroon lace underwear that I bought specifically for them. To be honest, I've completely replaced every scrap of my lingerie since meeting them.

"Fuck, this is sexy." Jepson slides his hands up my belly and cups my breasts, squeezing them together and burying his face into my cleavage. I toss my head back, my eyes on Jaxson, who strokes my hair as he stares down at me and his brother.

"Take your shirt off, baby." I make a show of pulling on the tucked ends of his button-down.

He works the buttons while I fumble with his belt and slide down the zipper of his slacks. I don't give him a second to think, slipping my hand inside his pants to knead his hardening cock. Jaxson takes in a deep breath, his eyes half-lidded as he peels off his shirt and tosses it behind the couch.

"Pants too," I moan as Jepson unfastens my bra and uses his teeth to tease and toy with my nipples.

Jaxson unbuttons his slacks and pushes them off his hips, his cock jutting out through the slit in his boxers. As many times as they have gone down on me—Jepson stripping his shirt so our bare chests touch every time, while Jaxson normally only lifts my skirt and removes my panties—neither has allowed me to take off their pants. So although I had a good idea how glorious their cocks would be, riding them fully clothed as we made out, seeing him erect and aching in front of me makes my mouth water.

I wrap my fingers around him at the same time

Jepson nuzzles my neck and speaks in a low, husky tone in my ear. "You want to wrap your lips around him, don't you?"

"Yes."

"Good, and while you're doing that, you're going to sit on my face and ride my tongue." He sucks my earlobe into his mouth and nibbles with his teeth. "Now get off these panties."

God, I love it when Jepson gets all growly alpha on me, especially since Jaxson is much more careful and nurturing. It's like between the two of them, they are the perfect man, fulfilling every romantic hero characteristic I've enjoyed watching in the movies.

I climb off Jepson's lap and stand up while he slides down on the couch to lie flat. At the same time, Jaxson helps me step out of my thong and kisses me until I'm breathless before guiding me to straddle Jepson's chest. This isn't the first time I've sat on his face. He loves sucking on my clit like this and moves me with forceful hands until I'm positioned just as he likes. One swipe of his tongue and I'm tossing my head back and reaching for Jaxson's swollen cock.

His body is equally beautiful, with hard-honed muscle and black and blue ink tiger eyes staring back at me from low on his non-existent belly.

He steps forward, gathering up my hair into a loose ponytail as I lick the precum dripping off the head. I open my mouth wide and take him as deep as possible, pleased when he groans low in his throat and tightens his hand in my hair. I feared he'd handle me too gently, but I'm thrilled he's taking his pleasure from me and showing me how he likes to be touched, wrapping his fingers around mine and stroking hard and faster.

Once I establish a rhythm with my hand and mouth that he likes, he reaches down and plucks at my nipples while Jepson plunges his tongue inside me. I moan and whine around Jaxson's cock as Jepson works my pussy perfectly, knowing how long to tease my clit with his teeth before lapping his tongue in long strokes over my hole. He grips my hips and grinds me against his mouth, his jaw covered with just enough stubble to provide delicious friction against my labia.

Pulling my mouth off of Jaxson, I continue to work him with my hand while gasping for air, my orgasm on the verge of crashing over. "Oh god, oh damn, yes, right there..."

My thighs clasp around Jepson's head as he wrings every quivering pulse of my climax out of me with only his talented tongue.

"That's our girl. I fucking love having you come down my throat," Jepson says as he maneuvers me down to straddle his chest. "How's her mouth, Jaxson?"

As if reminding me I have a job to do, I lean to the side and reclaim him between my lips, sucking him harder now that my brain isn't torn between his and my pleasure.

"Like heaven." Jaxson's hand tightens in my hair again.

Jepson reaches around me and unfastens his pants, shimmying his hips underneath me. I hear rather than see the foil condom wrapper tear open, rather impressed with Jepson's stealthy skill.

He latches on to my nipple, his fingers digging into my ass cheeks before wrapping around my hips. "Turn around and ride my cock, sweetheart. Jaxson, move to between my feet."

Jaxson pops free of my lips and helps me change position with Jepson, both of us doing exactly as his bossy brother directs.

He presses one knee between Jepson's feet and leans down, cupping my face and tilting my head back to claim my lips. "You are pure perfection, Maryanne. How do you feel?"

"Loved."

"You are loved, baby. So very much."

Jepson teases me from behind, dragging the head of his cock back and forth through my slick pussy lips, coating himself in my arousal before sliding in an inch. He sits up and grips my hips, his lips pressed between my shoulder blades. "Are you ready for me, sweetheart?"

"Yes."

He pulls me down hard on him, a gasp forced from my lips. "Oh god."

He sucks in his breath and hisses through clenched teeth. "Fuck, your pussy is amazing."

A tremor skitters through my limbs as he lays his hand flat between my shoulders and pushes me forward until I'm once again at eye level with Jaxson's cock. I wrap my fingers around him and take him deep, determined to give him as much pleasure as he and his brother have given me over the last month.

Jaxson threads his fingers in my hair and pumps his hips with determination, chasing his release while Jepson works me from underneath. My body radiates pleasure through my veins, every nerve ending sparking to life as the three of us moan, groan, and pant through our shared experience. Part of me can't believe I'm doing this. The other part wonders how I'll ever live without the two of them in my life.

Is this temporary? I don't know. They don't make me feel anything other than cherished and adored, but how can a relationship like this last?

It doesn't matter. I'm going to enjoy them and myself for as long as possible, in whatever way possible, putting my heart and body in their capable hands. As Jaxson said, I'm doing what feels good and not worrying about what's going on outside these walls while we're doing it.

Jepson reaches around and rubs my clit with one hand, the other wrapped around my waist as he thrusts up into me at a hurried pace. Soon all three of us are on the edge, Jaxson declaring his need to release.

"Maryanne, I'm going to come."

Jepson growls behind me. "Are you going to swallow every drop my brother has to give you, sweetheart?"

I nod, sticking my tongue out with my mouth open wide. He takes over, jerking himself to completion in three more short strokes. As soon as he is done, Jepson bands his arm around my chest and pulls me up so that my back is pressed to his chest. He continues to pump into me from underneath, his fingertip circling my clit until my orgasm crests over the edge. My pussy clamps down on his cock, which makes him release, his arms tightening around my midsection and his teeth clamping down on my shoulder.

I open my eyes to find Jaxson smiling down at me and caressing my cheek with his fingers. Then he leans forward, claiming my lips in a gentle kiss infused with love. "You okay?"

"Yes."

"Happy birthday, baby."

Chapter Eleven
Jepson

Fuck me, I haven't come that hard in a long time.

Maybe it was the month of foreplay, or maybe it is something more.

I told Jaxson yesterday that I'm falling in love with her, but I didn't understand what that meant until right now. I will shrivel up and die without her. She owns my heart and doesn't even know it yet.

Jaxson helps Maryanne to her feet and then swings her up into his arms, sitting down on the cushion next to me with her cradled in his lap. I sit up and pull off the condom, tying a knot in the end. "I'll be right back."

Pulling up my pants, I jog into the bathroom and clean up and then stop by a drawer in the kitchen, pulling out a spare set of keys. I walk back into the living room to find them snuggling with a blanket draped loosely over them. Jaxson is whispering in her ear, and I wonder if he's telling her how much he loves her.

He does. I can tell by the look in his eye that he's

head over heels crazy for her—just like me—only he has the emotional maturity to know how to express it.

I sit next to him and pull her legs into my lap, rubbing her bare feet. "Are you okay, sweetheart?"

"More than okay."

"Will you stay with us tonight?"

"Yes." She reaches out and squeezes my arm.

"And Sunday night?" I arch my brow.

"What about Sunday night?"

"We fly out around noon tomorrow and have to leave here at ten, but since we're playing an early game, I think we're scheduled to be home Sunday night. We'd love for you to be here when we get home."

Her smile widens. "Text me as soon as you land and I'll start driving."

"Or you use your key and be here waiting for us, preferably wearing nothing." I grin and hand her a set of key fobs. "This one is for the gate. This one is for the garage. And this is for the house, although we rarely lock that door."

"You're giving me keys to your house?" She giggles. "Am I moving in?"

"I'd be okay with that. What do you think, Jaxson?"

"Sounds like a perfect arrangement to me." He presses his lips to her cheek.

"I'm guessing this isn't a one-time thing, then?" She looks between the two of us.

I lean forward, putting my nose to hers. "I'm crazy about you, and nothing would make me happier than to come home to you night after night."

"Same, baby." Jaxson chuckles. "For the first time in my life, I'm in complete agreement with my brother."

"Aw, come on, man. It's not the first time." I pull back and shake my head.

"True. You have more good ideas than I care to admit." He gives me a meaningful look, and I know he's talking about right now. We wouldn't be here if I hadn't pushed for this to be a reality. Not because he didn't want it too, but because he thinks I'm unwilling to share with him. I know this more now than ever because I'm talking to a therapist twice a week—a minor fact he still doesn't know. I plan to tell him soon, especially since the therapist thinks a few couple-like therapy sessions would do both of us a lot of good, but I needed to start this on my own without judgment.

Of course, Jaxson would be supportive, but that would've pissed me off a month ago.

Now? I want to be the best version of myself I can be for me and my future, which hopefully includes Maryanne.

"I don't think we're watching a movie tonight." I lean in and claim her lips. She frames my face with her delicate hands, kissing me back with equal amounts of love and need. I slide my hand under the blanket and up her thigh, noting Jaxson's hand is already covering her breast and playing with her nipples. Slipping two fingers between her legs, I groan when she spreads her thighs for me, wordlessly granting me access to her pussy.

She surprised me when she walked into the living room and straddled my lap without a word. I mean, I had full intention of getting us to this very point sometime tonight, but I thought it would take some careful maneuvering and gentle persuasion. Whatever Jaxson did with her downstairs to get her rip-roaring ready to go, I salute him and his effort. Tonight has turned out better than even I expected.

Next step—forever.

I slowly pump my fingers in and out of her, my thumb drawing lazy circles around her clit. Her eyes flutter close as she lets her head roll to the side, her hips moving in tiny gyrations as she rides my hand. "Jaxson needs to feel you come on his cock."

"Yes," she moans, reaching her arm over her head to run her fingers along his scalp—both of our hair is too short to pull.

I hand Jaxson a condom and then pull the blanket off her, revealing her smooth, luscious body to my greedy gaze. "Fuck, Maryanne, you are so beautifully breathtaking. I can't believe you're mine."

"Ours," Jaxson corrects me.

"Sorry," I grin and nod. "I mean ours."

Scooting back, I pull her against me and kiss her hard, my hands and fingers sliding over her curves while Jaxson sheathes himself. "On your hands and knees, sweetheart."

She bites her lip and drops to her hands, bowing down in front of me with her ass in the air. Jaxson kneels behind her, looming over her and trailing kisses over her ass and back before sliding his fingers inside her. I know by the way she gasps, her eyes rolling back in her head.

"So warm and wet," he says.

"Absolutely perfect for us," I agree.

Maryanne smiles and cups me through my slacks. "Are you going to feed me again?"

"It won't be a strawberry this time." I undo my slacks and fist my cock, stroking slowly as she lowers her head and engulfs me with her slick, hot mouth. Groaning as she takes over, I gather her hair and hold it in my clenched fist at the same time Jaxson slides deep inside her.

"Oh, damn," my brother hisses, his blue eyes vibrant in the dimly lit room.

"She's amazing, right?" I say with a low moan. "Everything we want and more."

He nods, his fingers curling around her waist as he pumps his hips in a slow, steady rhythm.

Our whole lives I've been the talker, he's been the listener.

I'm the joker, while he's the thoughtful one.

I'm the hothead, and he's the sensible one.

I'm the instigator, and he's the mediator.

I believe between the two of us, we can be everything Maryanne wants and needs.

Jaxson reaches around and plays with her clit while I toy with her nipples, the three of us taking our time to enjoy the feel of each other. Only when Maryanne tenses up and Jaxson groans do I know they're close to coming. I pull her off my cock and kiss her deeply, Jaxson banding his arms around her chest as I did earlier, and pumping his hips hard and fast as she cries out her release. Seconds later, he's growling and burying his face into her neck with words of love and devotion as he shoots his load.

Maryanne can barely hold herself erect, slumping in Jaxson's arms with heavy-lidded eyes as she smiles sheepishly at me. I chuckle. "You look like the cat that ate the canary."

"You feel better—and make me feel better—than I imagined. Not even in my wildest fantasies did I think it would be like this."

"Can you handle an eternity of this?"

Her eyes open wide and lock with mine. "Can you?"

Jaxson and I take two seats next to each other at the back of the plane, talking low so no one overhears us.

"To be honest, I don't understand the switch that has flipped with you. Ever since we got in trouble in Nashville, you've been acting differently. If anyone was going to break the coach's curfew, I thought it would be you. Over a month of no clubs and no women?"

I shrug. "I've been otherwise motivated."

He frowns. "I believe—no, I know—you're in love with Maryanne. So, is that it? Did meeting her change everything for you?" Jaxson has been gently picking a fight with me since we left the house this morning with Maryanne sleeping in his bed.

"Yes, I'm in love with her. I told you that two days

ago. So are you. But she's not the reason, or at least she's not the only reason."

Jaxson sighs and leans his head back. "I'm too tired to play twenty questions with you."

"I've been seeing a therapist," I begrudgingly admit, surprised at how good it feels to say it out loud. Until this moment, it was my dirty secret that I'd only recently shared with Maryanne.

My brother pins me with his bright blue eyes, lines forming in his furrowed brow. Considering therapy in our family—specifically our father's feelings about the legitimacy of talking through your feelings—is a four-letter word, I know Jaxson is confused. Especially since I've spent a majority of my life hell-bent against it "Since when?"

"Right after Nashville. A couple of days after Coach pulled us into his office, he called me in the middle of practice. Pretty much, he told me if the team was forced to choose between us, they were going to choose you, and it was up to me to change his mind. He mandated eight therapy sessions minimum, two a week for a month, to prove I'm willing to do the work on myself."

Jaxson stares at the tiny screen embedded in the headrest in front of him and says nothing.

"What, man?"

He shakes his head. "I didn't say anything."

"No, but you're thinking it. Say it," I snap.

"I'm proud of you."

That was not what I expected him to say, and yet, I should expect nothing less from him. "Thanks."

"Do you find talking to them helpful?"

"Yeah, I do, and I think it would be good for us to hash out some childhood bullshit together."

"Like when mom died?" Jaxson says these words so low, I barely hear him.

"Yeah."

He nods. "I'd like that."

We sit in silence for a few minutes, staring at the game images playing for us on the screens.

Jaxson chuckles.

"What?"

"I'm used to volatile, manipulative, selfish Jepson. It's going to take a while to get used to this new, selfless version."

"What makes you think I'm selfless? Nothing has changed, except for maybe the volatility part."

"How do you explain last night, then? It's been your idea to share Maryanne the entire time. I expected at some point you would turn her off of me—I've been waiting for it—and then last night happened. You know it's exhausting waiting for you to fuck me over."

I close my eyes and count to ten, one of the many techniques the therapist has given me to control my anger. "I manipulated the entire scenario last night, Jaxs, except this time I did it for good versus evil."

I arch my brow. "As far as selfish versus selfless goes, I still am and probably will always be the same selfish bastard you've known and tolerated. The truth is, I knew from the beginning that if we force Maryanne to choose, she will choose you every time. You're a much better version of me any day, which is why I get so angry some-times. I don't know if I've ever really been mad at you, but I get angry with myself sometimes when I look at you and think about who I should've been."

Jaxson has his eyes down on his lap. "You're not mad at me for Mom?"

"Why would I be mad at you for Mom?" I say with genuine confusion. I know he feels guilty about that day, but I don't know why he would think I would be angry about it.

"Because, instead of sitting with her and saying good-bye, they tethered you to me to keep me alive."

I shift in my seat, so I'm facing him the best that I can in these tiny ass chairs, and kick him softly with the toe of my shoe. "Mom was dead when we got to the hospital. They might've had her on life support, but she was brain-dead before they pulled her out of that car. Even at four-teen, I understood and was more terrified of losing my brother, too. I've never been mad at you for that day, but I've hated myself for a long time because of the last things I said to our mother before y'all left. I knew something was wrong with you. I knew it was serious. I said horrible things before she left, and then I wished horrible things while you were gone. I'll never be able to take that back, but I'm trying to learn how to forgive myself."

He shakes his head. "We should've talked about this twelve years ago. Then I could've saved you years of self-loathing."

"Told me what?"

"When we first pulled away from the school, mom

was ranting about how she was going to chew your ass when you got home. And then she was going to make you bake cookies and spend time with her while I rested. She said that if you felt she was playing favorites, that meant she wasn't doing her job to make sure you felt loved."

Tears well up in my eyes, and I can't control them as they fall silently down my cheeks. I grab my sunglasses off of my collar and slide them on my face, leaning my face against the rest facing him and the window only. "Fuck. I did and didn't need to know that."

Jaxson also grabs his sunglasses and slides them on his face, shaking his head. "We should've talked about all this shit a long fucking time ago."

I feel the need to cry and let loose all the anger, sadness, and frustration I've been carrying with me over the years, but a metal tube at thirty thousand feet while surrounded by my teammates and coaches is not the place to do it.

"Back to me being a selfish bastard..."

Jaxson chuckles.

"You and I—our bond is forever. Now, all I want is for you and Maryanne to be happy, but I think we can be happy together."

He nods. "After last night, I agree."

"From this moment on we work as a team, doing whatever we have to do to make a happy home with her."

Jaxson draws in a deep breath and lets it out slowly. "Whatever it takes to make her happy."

Chapter Twelve
Jaxson

The coaching staff stands in the middle of the visitor's locker room in Seattle's stadium, the room filled with somber silence. We got our asses handed to us today, losing by over twenty-four points. It is by far our worse defeat in a few years, and embarrassing.

"We expected today's game to be our toughest of the season. Seattle is the team to beat this year, but I know we are fundamentally better than them in every position. I bear the blame for this loss, and should have seen this coming after our loss to Philly two weeks ago," Mike Monroe says calmly.

Daniel Scott steps forward. "No, Mike. We're a team, a family, and the front office has been holding on too tightly. That's my fault. You guys need a break. A month ago, I asked for your best and I feel you've been giving it. Today is a reflection of what happens when it's all work and no play. We are all wound tight, and you need some time to cut loose and relax. Effective immediately, the team curfew is lifted and Monday family days are reinstated. We're still going from seven to seven Wednesday through Sunday, but I'm hoping you can decompress without ending up in jail or as headline fodder."

Mike Monroe nods. "You guys are doing a great job. Today was a bad day. Take a few days off, decompress, and come back ready to dominate on Wednesday."

Rex packs up his bag next to Jepson and me. "We're free."

"Thank god," I mutter.

"Want to go out tomorrow night?"

Jepson nods. "Yeah. Let's head up to Denver."

"What?" I snap. We spent the entire flight here talking about how things were going to be different and the first sign of light he pulls this shit?

My brother pins me with bright blue eyes. "Trust me, she'll love it."

"Absolutely not." I shove stuff in my bag and hoist it on my shoulder, my fists clenched at my side.

"What's going on?" Rex looks at us. "Who are you talking about?"

"Our girlfriend." Jepson keeps his voice low so only the three of us can hear.

"No shit?" He seems to contemplate this and then shrugs. "Okay, then."

"We are not taking Maryanne to a fucking strip club." I hiss, leaning in aggressively to emphasize my point.

"Maryanne Merryweather?" Rex coughs, but we ignore him. They met a week ago when she started working on his charity involvement with Paladin Place.

"She wants to go, Jaxs. We talked about it a while ago. With her psychology background and fascination with human interaction, I told her she'd love the people watching there."

"Yeah, but who's going to be watching her?" I had no idea I could rock this level of possessiveness, and I don't want her anywhere near the men who frequent those establishments. And to be honest, I don't want her to see us there. What if Jepson pulls an asshole move, and she's there to witness it? Our relationship is new, fragile, and not open to fuck around and find out.

"We will be." He looks at me like I'm crazy.

"No." I walk out of the locker room to the bus, taking a seat next to Rylie Reynolds. If Jepson pushes me, I might punch him in the face.

Geez, how the tables have turned in such a short amount of time.

Jepson seems to realize I'm on the edge of reason, so he and Rex sit a couple of seats ahead of me on the bus. By the time we're boarding the plane, I'm super pissed because Jepson sent Maryanne a preemptive text via our group chat that continues to blow up my phone.

> Jepson: Hey, sweetheart. Did you see the game?

> Maryanne: Hi you. I did. I'm sorry the team lost. The commentators weren't very nice to Declan.

Jepson: Yeah, it was an off night for us and the quarterback always takes the brunt of the blame. He also takes a majority of the glory. It's part of being the team captain. Do you understand the game?

Maryanne: A little, but you'll have to explain it to me someday.

Jepson: While cuddling on the couch?

Maryanne: Of course. Where's Jaxson?

Jepson: He's mad at me right now, but you'll make him feel better when we get home. Are you there waiting for us now?

Maryanne: Yes, I am. Why is he mad? Babe?

Jepson: They lifted our curfew, and I want to take you up to Denver to Diamonds and Pearls Cabaret for your birthday tomorrow night. He's not on board.

Maryanne: Jaxson? Baby? Why does it bother you?

Gritting my teeth, I begrudgingly respond.

I don't see any reason to subject you to that environment, especially when we're just starting this relationship.

Jepson: He thinks I'm going to act a fool and ruin your opinion of us.

Maryanne: Are you?

Jepson: No. I'm not going to risk losing
you, but he's seen me do too many
stupid things over the years to trust me.

Maryanne: I guess I'll have to prove to
you both that I'm not giving up on us
that easily.

Sinking into my seat, I close my eyes, my mind and body infused with a small sense of relief.

She won't give up on us that easily. Thank god.

A body plops down in the chair next to me. "We have a lifetime of you watching over me, Jaxs, but you have to trust me. I'm not going to do anything to fuck up things with Maryanne—for either of us. I promise."

"You better not." I don't open my eyes. I can't look at him right now. Instead, I pray for patience.

He sighs, settling in next to me. "You'll see."

Three hours and a solid nap later, we pull into our garage and park next to Maryanne's five-year-old Subaru. The relief I feel knowing she's here is palpable, and the tightness in my chest since Jepson sprung Denver on me releases. We enter the house to music playing, Maryanne walking around the corner in a short terry cloth bathrobe. "Welcome home."

I drop my bag, catching her as she flings herself into my arms. She throws her legs around my waist and peppers my face with kisses, my cock instantly hard, my sole focus to bury myself deep inside of her. "I missed you, baby."

"I missed you too," she whispers in my ear.

I set her down, surprised to not find Jepson standing

beside us. Maryanne seems to notice this too, looking around to find him several feet away, leaning his ass against the breakfast bar with his hands shoved in his pockets.

"Hi." Maryanne slides her hand down my chest and over my erection before taking the six steps away to walk into his chest.

"Hey, sweetheart." He pulls her into his arms, kissing the top of her head, but keeps his eyes on me. "Were you about to take a shower?"

"Yes, but I thought I'd wait for you to come home." She smiles at him and then looks over her shoulder at me. "That is, if you want to take a shower with me?"

"Why don't you and Jaxs take one? I'll fix us a snack. I'm starving."

"We have tiramisu and leftover Italian food."

"Perfect." He leans down and kisses her neck, whispering in her ear.

She nods and steps away from him, taking my hand and leading me to the stairs without saying a word.

"What did he say?" I follow her, too tired and too turned on to fight his blatant manipulation.

"He said you need me right now," she says as we walk into my bathroom, pulling the sash on her robe and letting the sides fall naturally apart.

My hungry eyes take in every inch of her. It's been less than forty-eight hours since I was last inside her lush body, and yet it feels like an eternity. "I do need you. I really do."

"You have me." She works the buttons on my shirt as

I unbuckle my belt, both of us making quick work of my clothes. In seconds, I have warm water spraying down on us, my hands cradling her ass and supporting her thighs as she spreads wide for me. I lift and pin her against the tile wall, sliding deep inside her slick body without a condom.

"Oh, damn. You feel so good." I fuse our mouths, kissing her with all the love and need coursing through my limbs. Jepson was one hundred percent correct—I'm worried he's going to fuck things up for us. I know he loves her, but sometimes I don't think he can control his self-sabotaging impulses.

"I'm on the pill." She gasps as I thrust up my hips a little harder.

"What?" I grunt, my mouth buried in her neck.

"Birth control. We didn't talk about it Friday night, but I'm on it, so you don't have to worry about coming inside of me."

"Are you sure?"

"Yes, baby. I want you to."

Something about shooting my seed inside of her, the image of her round with my child, brings me to the edge of release within seconds. I can't hold back, my balls tightening up, cum shooting up my shaft. "Ah, fuck." I clench my teeth and pump my hips, filling her and silently wishing we were making a baby. I'd love nothing more than for her to have my child.

Damn. I've never had thoughts like that before.

"Sorry. I couldn't hold back." I pull my face back to look her in the eye.

She smiles sweetly, cupping my face in her hands. "I like you desperate to be inside of me.

I slip out of her and set her on her feet, sitting her on the tile bench. "Spread your legs for me."

Maryanne leans back and spreads her knees, my cum sliding out of her pussy as the rain-head showers down on my back. I kneel and slip my fingers inside of her, stroking her g-spot while rubbing her clit with my thumb until she's moaning and riding my fingers. Lowering my mouth onto her plump clit, I suck it against my teeth, rewarded when she bucks her hips against my lips.

"Oh, yes." She moans, her gyrations becoming erratic. "Right there."

"Come for me, baby."

"Oh god. Yes, Jaxson." She cries out her release, her pussy clamping down on my fingers, pulsing and begging for my cock, which is half-hard again. I kiss her thighs and then trail my tongue up her belly to her breasts, sucking her nipples into my mouth before claiming her lips again. I suppose this would be called a quickie, but I feel so much more relaxed after spending less than fifteen minutes with her. "I'm glad you're home."

"Me too."

"About Diamonds and Pearls."

I sigh, standing up and pulling her to her feet.

"Jepson and I talked about it weeks ago and if I knew it would upset you, I wouldn't have told him I want to go."

"Do you want to go?"

She bites her lip and nods. "Very much. I've always

been curious, but I'm too much of a chicken to go by myself. With you and Jepson, I feel safe. He promised that if we ever went, and I was uncomfortable in any way, he'd take me home immediately—no questions asked. You know I'm fairly sheltered, but I have so many things I'm curious about and hoped when I met the right man, I could explore my wild side. Well, now I have two men who I know will protect me, no matter what."

I frame her face in my hands and kiss her forehead, then the tip of her nose, before placing a chaste kiss against her lips. "If you—and I mean YOU—want to go, then we'll go."

Shaking my head, I chuckle. "I swear, between you and Jepson, I'm never going to win an argument."

She wraps her arms around my waist and presses her cheek to my chest. "This wasn't an argument. This was you taking care of me, and I love you for it."

Hearing the word love roll off her tongue so easily makes my heart expand in my chest. I turn the water off, recognizing that no soap touched either of our bodies, and wrap my arms around her back. "I love you too."

Chapter Thirteen
Maryanne

I love you, too.

I love you, too?

I love you, too!

Yes, I feel loved by their touch, their words, and their thoughtful care of me, but to have the words said to me for the first time at nearly thirty-three years old feels surreal.

And yet, I one hundred percent believe him.

Jaxson wraps a towel around me and then another one around his waist before grabbing my robe, also sliding it over my arms. "I guess I have to thank Jepson for giving me some alone time with you."

"Granted, I haven't known either of you for very long, but I feel like he is trying to be better."

Jaxson's brow furrows. "What do you know?"

I bite my lip. Shit, have I said too much? "A week ago, he mentioned he's talking to a therapist, which was something he would never have done before, and feels like it's helping him."

"Son of a bitch." Jaxson leans his ass against the counter. "He told you before he told me."

"I think he told me because I used to be one, and therefore felt safe. As you said before, your father isn't big into talking, so I can only imagine what he would think about therapy." I place my hands on his eight-pack and press my breast against his chest. "Please don't be mad."

He shakes his head. "I'm not mad—just surprised, that's all."

I rest my chin on his sternum and smile up at him. "I'm glad you're home. Your next game is here, right?"

"Yes. We'll be sleeping in our beds every night for the next ten days, and we have Monday and Tuesday off this week."

"I have appointments during the day, but I'm all yours at night time."

"You should move some of your stuff in. We have a third room that you can make your own so you can have your own space when you need it."

I sigh. "This is moving fast."

He shakes his head. "Technically, we've been dating for a month, but I understand what you mean."

It's Monday night and a car service has picked us up at the house. I'm both excited and nervous about the gentleman's club. I know what I look like to most people. I'm short, cute, and curvy, and although I have all the makings of a voluptuous bombshell, I don't give off that vibe no matter what I'm wearing or how sultry I do my hair and makeup.

It's this vibe that I think first attracted Jaxson and Jepson, but for two very different reasons. For Jaxson, it's my perceived sweetness that makes him feel like I would be a safe bet, considering I match his sweetness. I also think that's why he's worried about tonight.

For Jaxson, I think deep down he likes the idea of corrupting me while encouraging my spicy wild side.

Fortunately or unfortunately, as the case may be, I have fantasized about being corrupted for a long time.

Why can't I be both sweet and spicy?

As discussed this morning, we picked up Rex and Rylie on our way to Denver. Rex knows I'm dating both Jepson and Jaxson and doesn't think it's odd at all. Rylie, whom I haven't met yet, thinks I'm a friend who is lucky enough to have friends taking her out for her birthday. Considering I doubt Jepson or Jaxson will keep their hands off me tonight, I doubt he'll believe that fib for long.

I wish we could've invited London, but considering Deacon and his position in the organization, I didn't want to risk any potential fallout from my fraternization with football players, or his opinion of the Masters twins dating his fiancé's best friend.

Because of my talent for putting people at ease quickly and being somebody people feel they can open up to, it doesn't take long for the five of us to fall into friendly conversation spanning a variety of topics. Rex regales us with stories from his childhood that have me laughing so hard, I suspect my mascara is smudged. He was not only the class clown, but his family's prankster, and after a few stories, I understand why he and Jepson became such good friends.

Rylie tells me about his daughter, who is his pride and joy, and I can tell when we work on his charity, it will involve mentoring kids. I guess his ex-wife, his child's mother, gave up all parental rights, which I can't even fathom. His daughter is with her maternal grandparents this weekend, which is the only reason he is out with us tonight.

There are two stops on tonight's agenda—Del Frisco's Steakhouse and then Diamonds and Pearls Cabaret. After an amazing dinner, I feel like a princess being escorted by four large men into the nearly empty club. I guess it's early, even for a Monday night, which Jepson prefers. Rex and Rylie already feel like big brothers, and the inappropriate touches Jepson and Jaxson made at the dinner table have made our relationship blatantly clear. Both men kissed me multiple times without thinking twice about our audience. I doubt everyone we meet will be so open-minded, but neither of the men with us seem to care.

We take one small booth and a small table in the VIP area to the side of center stage. Jepson excuses himself, walking up to one of the waitresses as Jaxson and I slide into the booth. The waitress glances over his shoulder at us and smiles, nods, and then walks away. At the same time, a beautiful long-haired blonde dancer waves and pulls a tall, slender man behind her, approaching Jepson, who in turn brings them back to our tables.

The thin man smiles sheepishly at the assembled men.

Jepson pats him on the back. "James here is a huge Rangers fan."

As the guys introduce themselves and shake hands, Jepson pulls me to his side. "Baby, this is Carrie. She's in law school at DU."

Carrie has a body most women would kill to have as well as a beautiful face. "Hi."

"It's nice to meet you. This one needs a good woman in his life to keep him honest." She elbows Jepson and then points to her man. "That's my husband, James. He fangirls over the guys every time they come in. Most of the boyfriends and husbands do."

"Are all the dancers in relationships?" I ask.

"Most are. Would you like to meet some of them?"

"Sure."

Carrie grabs my hand and looks Jepson in the eye. "No boys allowed."

"I know." He rolls his eyes and then winks at me. "Have fun."

The dressing room is posh with makeup tables and

couches, showers and lockers. Four ladies are touching up their makeup and chatting about one of their kid's second-grade classroom drama.

"And then this helicopter mom had the nerve to get in my Tara's face, and you know it took everything within me not to get violent." A beautiful woman with long reddish blonde hair and dark brown eyes waves her hand in the air to demonstrate her point.

Another woman shakes her head and grumbles, "I know that."

"Hey ladies. This is Jepson Masters' woman." Carrie puts her hands on my shoulders. "You know, he never said your name."

"It's Maryanne."

"Hey, Maryanne." One woman stands and shakes my hand. "Are you a dancer too?"

I laugh. "No. I'm not nearly ballsy or beautiful enough to do something like this."

"It's not about being beautiful, honey. It's about being confident in your skin."

"And convincing everyone else you're a badass boss bitch that owns that pole," another one chuckles.

Carries points to each woman. "Married with two kids. Engaged, no kids. Boyfriend and boyfriend."

"Don't your men get jealous?" I'm in awe. Their confidence is inspiring.

The reddish-blonde with the little girl shakes her head. "I've been with my husband for eleven years. I only started doing this three years ago. I wanted to send our kids to private school, and while my husband makes decent money, tuition is almost twenty grand per kid per year. I can do this a handful of nights a month and cover their tuition, books, uniforms, and after-school activities. Do you have any idea how much ballet shoes and swim lessons cost?"

I shake my head.

"Anyway, all my husband cares about is that I'm safe while working. I don't think he'd be cool with me working anywhere else, but this club is high end and the security staff is excellent."

"My fiancé became a bouncer here, just so he could watch over me. He's not jealous, but very protective," a brunette adds.

"My husband is an ER doctor, so most nights he's on call. He comes to watch me when he can. Between his student loans and my law school tuition, this is paying off all of our debt. Plus, it's a great workout." Carrie grins.

"That's so smart."

"I do it because I love it." A petite woman with dark black hair eyes me through her reflection in the mirror while applying a set of false lashes. "I love shaking my ass and getting paid for it. I used to be a Hooters girl, and the simple fact is, if a man is going to be a pig, he's going to be a pig anywhere. At least here I'm protected, and it pays well."

"So—" the brunette crosses her legs "—how did you and Jepson hook up?"

"Uh, well, I'm the project manager for the Rangers' charity outreach. I help the players get hooked up with different organizations, set up events, stuff like that."

"That's how you met Jepson?"

"That's how I met all of them." I blush and look down at my shoes.

Carrie sucks in her breath. "Are you with all four of them?"

"Four?" someone gasps.

"No." I shake my head. "Not all four of them. Two of them."

One woman giggles while another one cackles. "I guess you're the badass boss bitch in the room tonight!"

My blush deepens, my cheeks burning with it.

"We should get you on stage to dance for them." Carrie smiles.

My eyes grow wide. "Jaxson would be very unhappy if I did that."

Her mouth drops open. "The twins? Really? I've always wondered about him."

"About Jaxson?"

"Yeah, he's so quiet compared to his brother. Broody. He never blatantly watches the dancers and most of the time sits in the chair facing away from the main stage. You can tell he's here as his brother's wingman, and not because he likes the dancers."

"If you want a few tips, we can send you home with the tools tonight to drive them wild!" Carrie offers.

I grin. "I'll take them."

Twenty minutes later, two of the dancers have been on and off stage, and Carrie has given me a decent workout running me through a handful of moves. A waitress walks in and announces that my men are worried and want to know if I'm coming back. I thank the ladies, exchange numbers with Carrie for a future lunch date, and am surprised to see the club has doubled in patrons since we walked in.

"Are you okay?" Jaxson asks as Jepson slides out of the booth to make room for me between them.

"Yes. They are fascinating women."

Jepson slides next to me and puts his hand on my thigh under the table. "Told you so."

I'm not sure if that statement was for me or to reassure his brother.

Jaxson wraps his cool fingers over the back of my neck. "Why are you sweating, baby?"

I lean in and whisper in his ear. "Carrie showed me a few dance moves for later, in case one of you wants a lap dance."

Jaxson's eyes flash with heat and he leans over me to talk at Jepson. "When can we leave?"

I giggle, placing one hand on each of their legs, sliding my fingers teasingly up and down the inside of their thighs, hidden from view by the table.

Jepson grabs my hand and places it directly on his hard cock. "We'll leave as soon as Maryanne says she's ready to go."

I suck in my breath. "You know, Carrie said I could give you a private show in one of the rooms in the back."

Jaxson shakes his head. "Supposedly, there are no cameras back there, but we wouldn't risk fucking you someplace public—just in case."

"Unless public sex is a kink you're interested in exploring?" Jepson asks.

"Maybe someday." I bat my lashes.

He lifts my chin with his finger and presses his lips to mine. "Whatever you want, baby, we're here to give it to you. With two men who love and adore you, we should never leave you wanting for anything."

I flex my fingers over both of their hardening cocks, my pussy tingling with need. "Let's watch Carrie dance and then we can go."

Chapter Fourteen
Jepson

Jaxson gets antsier every minute Maryanne is out of view in the dressing room.

"Will you relax?" I take a sip of my whiskey and soda and confirm the second car, the one I booked to make sure Rex and Rylie get back to Spring City whenever they want. I'm pretty sure after spending time here, Jaxson and I are going to want Maryanne all to ourselves on the forty-five minute drive home.

"Where is she?" he grumbles as more patrons enter the club. He doesn't like crowds, and I know this. Neither do I, really. I prefer coming early and during the week to avoid the riff-raff. This is a high-end club, which means money, not all of which is respectable. A lot of professional football, hockey, baseball, and basketball players come here, as well as doctors, lawyers, and even the occasional politician, but I'm sure they aren't the only corrupt ones here on any given night.

I grab the waitress. "Could you do me a favor and check on our female friend? She's in the dressing room with Carrie."

"Sure."

Rex, Rylie, and James are at a small table between us and the stage, but they are busy bullshitting about one thing or another and not paying attention to the dancers. I think Rylie comes out with us because he doesn't know what to do with his limited free time. Technically a bachelor, he hasn't lived the single life in six years, and isn't interested in dating as a single father. Rex, that poor bastard, has fallen in love with every woman he's ever slept with, which is always the wrong woman. He's gotten better about holding his feelings close since we started hanging out, mostly because I tease him mercilessly about it every time. He's a good guy and deserves a good woman, but his picker is horrible.

He's right up there with Aggie, except Rex has been smart enough to not marry any of them.

Maryanne walks out from the dressing rooms with rosy cheeks. I hop out of the booth and let her slide in next to Jaxson, noting the pink flush on her cleavage.

"Are you okay?" Jaxson asks.

"Yes. They are really fascinating women." She grabs her champagne flute and takes a couple of sips.

I slide my hand onto her thigh under the table. "Told you."

That's more for Jaxson than it is for her.

"Why are you sweating, baby?" He ignores me.

She leans in and whispers in his ear. I can't hear her over the music, but whatever she says has Jaxson leaning over her to yell at me. "When can we leave?"

She giggles and places her hand high on my thigh, my cock instantly hardening.

Using the table to shield us, I slide her hand over my erection. "We'll leave as soon as Maryanne says she's ready to go."

She sucks in her breath. "You know, Carrie said I could give you a private show in one of the rooms in the back."

Jaxson shakes his head. "Supposedly, there are no cameras back there, but we wouldn't risk fucking you someplace public—just in case."

"Unless public sex is a kink you're interested in exploring?" I add.

"Maybe someday."

I lift her chin and press my lips to hers. "Whatever you want, baby, we're here to give it to you. With two men who love and adore you, we should never leave you wanting for anything."

She flexes her fingers and massages my cock through my slacks. "Let's watch Carrie dance and then we can go."

Twenty minutes later, we're saying our goodbyes.

"Happy birthday, Maryanne." Rex shakes her hand, but Rylie's eyes are glued to the chick wearing rainbow thigh highs and pigtails on stage. She's not a dancer I've seen before, not that I know all of them. Is that what he's into? Interesting. Not that I'm here to judge, but she isn't what I was expecting.

Once we're on the road with the privacy screen up between us and the driver, I pull Maryanne's legs onto my lap, her back cradled in Jaxson's arms. My hand slides up between her thighs, which she spreads easily for me, to stroke her silky panties. "Did you have fun, baby?"

"I did. This has been the most amazing birthday of my life. Thank you."

I grin at Jaxson. "How many times do you think we can get our birthday girl off before we get home?"

"At least three, I would think." He palms her breast through her top, pinching and plucking at her nipples.

I reach underneath her dress and pull off her panties, stuffing them in my pocket. Then I slide two fingers inside her, finding her hot, wet, and so ready to be fucked. "Did watching the dancers get you hot, baby?"

"A little, but mostly I fantasized about dancing for you, grinding down on your cocks, and driving you wild."

"Oh, you drive us wild plenty." I pump my fingers and circle her clit with my thumb as Jaxson claims her lips, kissing her with all the passion and need I feel right now. She's plenty worked up, and it takes nothing for her to roll her hips and ride my fingers, her climax building and breaking free quickly.

Jaxson swallows her cries of pleasure as I pull my fingers out and suck them clean. "That's one."

"My turn." My brother passes her to me and kneels on the floorboard in front of us. I pull her onto my lap and hike her skirt up to her waist. Jaxson pushes her thighs wide with his broad shoulders and descends on her pussy like a starved man while I fist a handful of her hair and plunge my tongue into her mouth. She tastes like champagne and cherries jubilee, although I think that's partially because of her flavored lip gloss. She digs her fingernails into my bicep, her other hand fisting Jaxson's collar as he tongue fucks her pussy.

Minutes and miles pass by before Maryanne moans, "Please, please, please."

"Please what, baby?" I growl into her ear.

"Please fuck me."

Jaxson's working his zipper at the same time his lips trail kisses down her thigh. With speed and efficiency, he fists his cock, lines up with her opening, and thrusts into her with such force, she slams back into my chest. I wrap my arms around her and grab hold of the backs of her knees, spreading and holding her wide as my brother fucks her hard. Jaxson closes his eyes and furiously pumps his hips as Maryanne tosses her head back onto my shoulder, her teeth clenched as a second orgasm rocks her body.

Knowing what it feels like to have her pussy walls milk my cock when she comes has me desperate to get inside of her. Jaxson grunts, the veins in his neck pulsing as he releases.

"Fuck me," he hisses, opening his eyes to look at the both of us. Glancing over his shoulder, he grabs a couple of tissues and pulls out, catching his cum as it trickles out of her. He pulls her off my lap and I take the opportunity to unbuckle my belt and slide my slacks down to my thighs.

We have fifteen miles until we reach the house, and we're running out of roadway. "Come here, baby."

Jaxson helps a dazed Maryanne straddle my lap. I thrust up inside her without preamble, holding her in my arms as she smiles drunkenly back at me.

"You both feel so good," she whines, as if the pleasure is too much.

"Can you come one more time for me?"

"I'll try."

With his pants done, Jaxson reaches around her and slides his hand between us, his middle fingertip finding her engorged clit. I rock her back and forth on my cock, chasing my release while hers builds again. We're exiting the interstate and pulling into our neighborhood when she buries her face into my neck, her third orgasm clamping down on my cock. That's all I need to send me over the edge. I wrap my arms around her tightly, my cock jumping inside her as I release my load.

The driver comes over the intercom. "Pulling up to the house now, sirs."

Maryanne pulls her face from my neck and sighs. "You two are amazing."

"Back at you, baby."

Jaxson pulls her off my lap and I tuck my cock in my pants right as the driver pulls to a stop in front of our gate. I hit the key fob and the gates open, letting him drive us up to the house. To make sure Maryanne avoids awkward eye contact with our driver, Jaxson opens the passenger side door and pulls her out with him without saying goodbye.

I'm not so lucky as the driver opens my door. I toss the used tissues in the wastebasket and pull out my phone, tipping the driver through the car service app. "Thanks for the ride."

The driver, who I'm sure is used to this kind of thing, nods without making eye contact. "Have a pleasant night, sir."

It's been a couple of grueling weeks on the field, but the team is doing well again, and I've had a couple of chances to play with the offensive line as a running back, scoring my first touchdown of my professional career. The coach is happy with my playing, although he felt the need to remind me I'm not out of the dog house yet.

It's Monday and Jaxson is on a date with Maryanne, something the two of us do every other week. This Monday is his, next Monday is mine, etcetera, etcetera. Our home life is working for now, although I feel like all of us are waiting to see what it will be like after the season is over. Our schedules are too crazy right now to feel truly settled.

Rex and I are on the north end picking up a couple of suits from the tailor before grabbing a couple of gourmet burgers, something Jaxson can't or shouldn't eat. My eyes instantly land on Aggie as soon as we walk in, and I walk over to him with a huge smile on my face. Rumor is his ex-wife set fire to most of his clothes, so I'm betting he's here to replace all of them now that his divorce is final.

Again, I didn't hear any of this from him. He keeps a very tight circle of friends, and I'm not part of it.

"Hey man. Are you finally replacing the suits Ellen turned into campfire kindling?" I walk up and slap Aggie's shoulder, my eyes instantly going to a blonde woman who could easily be a model.

Holy hell. I hadn't heard he was dating someone.

I quirk my brow, snark spewing from my lips before I can stop it. "Nice, Aggie. Way to get over that bitch of an ex-wife."

"It's not like that, so watch your mouth," Aggie mutters.

"Is she a dancer from the club?" I keep talking, my mouth on autopilot.

"Shut up before you say something you regret," he hisses.

She stands up and smooths her skirt, drawing my attention to the fact that her outfit is pure business professional. "No, I'm not a dancer."

"That's too bad." I flash my Sunday school smile. "You look familiar, though."

She narrows her eyes, clearly unimpressed by me. "You know, Mr. Masters, you should spend less time fighting with your brother at strip clubs and more time at your charitable organization—you know the one you're required to donate time and resources to monthly?"

A cannonball punches me in the gut as I realize how badly I just fucked up. Me and my big, self-sabotaging mouth!

She offers her hand and a few kind words to the tailor who in turn calls her Ms. Scott, and then walks out of the store without a second glance at any of us.

"Oh, shit," Rex hisses. "Please tell me that's not our boss's daughter."

Aggie's eyes are cold as he glances between me and Rex. "This isn't what it looks like, and I don't want to hear about this in the locker room tomorrow."

We shake our heads. "Nope. We never saw you."

"That works for me," he says as he walks out, leaving me there like a thoroughly scolded child.

Shit, I am a child. Fuck, I thought I was past doing stupid shit like this.

I exchange a glance with Rex who shakes his head and pulls a claim ticket out of his wallet. "You just can't help yourself, can you?"

"I'm telling you, man, sometimes it's like I'm outside my body watching the train wreck happen. What the fuck is wrong with me?"

"Don't know, but you better fucking fix it before they boot your ass from the team."

A few minutes later, I'm filled with regret as I exit the shop to find Aggie standing one door down watching Ms. Scott as she walks away.

"How much trouble am I in?" I say softly.

Aggie looks me dead in the eye. "In general, I'd say a lot. If you don't respect yourself, at least respect the jersey and the organization backing it. Your crap affects not only you but everyone else who dances within your sphere of influence—specifically your brother. If you're going to self-destruct, do it away from the team and our championship season."

I shove my hands in my pockets and hang my head low. "I'm trying, man. I just... I get stupid sometimes."

Aggie stares at me for a minute, his features softening. "Do you have a therapist you can talk to?"

I nod. "Yeah."

"Good. I find talking to someone helpful."

"Oh, yeah?" My head snaps up. I haven't told anyone other than Maryanne, Jaxson, and Rex about my therapy sessions, so I'm surprised to learn someone else is seeing one too.

"Yeah, man. There's no shame in talking through your crap. I'm glad you're seeing someone."

"Well, I didn't have much of a choice. The coach ordered it a while ago."

"However you get there, showing up is what is important."

Rex walks out of the store with two suits slung over his shoulder. "You want to grab a burger with us?"

Aggie raises his eyebrow. "Just a burger?"

I'm sure he expects me to suggest holding up a bank or robbing a pet store. At this point, no matter how hard I try on the field, it's my mouth that keeps everyone expecting the worst from me.

"Juicy beef between two buns next to a side of fries and maybe a milkshake. Nothing else." Rex points to an upscale grille across the parking lot as if to emphasize his point. "We're laying low for a while. No more rowdy nights out until we win a championship ring."

Aggie glances in the direction Ms. Scott walked away and then nods. "Okay."

Chapter Fifteen
Jaxson

Jepson hasn't been himself in weeks, although he's playing his heart out on the field. There's no more curfew, but outside of his and Maryanne's date night every other Monday, he's been a complete homebody.

No meals out, no club nights, no shenanigans—nothing.

I'm not the only one who has noticed it, either. He has Maryanne on edge, unwilling to talk about what's bothering him—worse, he keeps touting the "I'm fine, everything is fine" tract—which to me is worse than it was before.

It's week fifteen and we clenched our division with a win over Chicago. Even though the team is ready to celebrate, Jepson wants to go back to the hotel.

We ride the elevator together. "What the fuck, man? What is going on with you?"

"Nothing. I just don't feel like celebrating, okay?"

"No." I shake my head. "I mean, yes, I'm cool with not partying, not going out, not getting crazy, but I'm not cool with you not wanting to. This isn't like you, and you have me and Maryanne worried."

He sighs and slumps against the back wall of the elevator, his hand shoved deep into his pockets. "I don't want you to worry. It's just, remember how on Maryanne's birthday I told you I wouldn't do anything to fuck up things with her?"

"Yeah?"

"Well, there was an incident a couple of weeks ago, and now I'm afraid that maybe I won't be able to stop myself. Sometimes my mouth does things my brain can't control. I don't know where it comes from, and it seems like the safest bet for me is to keep my mouth shut and avoid people as much as possible."

I wrack my brain for what could have happened and when. "What was the incident?"

Jepson hangs his head. "Rex and I ran into Aggie and a pretty blonde, and I immediately said something stupid only to find out she was Deidre Scott."

His story leaves me with more questions than answers—like what were Aggie and Deidre Scott doing out together, where was this at, when, and what stupid thing did Jepson say—but I focus on what's important. "Has anybody from the organization talked to you?"

"No, but I have a sneaking suspicion Deacon knows about us and Maryanne."

"Why do you think that?" A lead ball drops in my belly. We know London knows because Maryanne told us, but supposedly she was going to keep it from Deacon to avoid backlash for all of us. Not that we've been overly cautious. Rex and Rylie know, but I'm not sure if anyone else does. If the rumor is going around, it hasn't come back to me yet.

"He hasn't said anything, but he's given me a look a couple of times that makes me wonder."

I chew on my lip and try to think back to any looks I've gotten. Playing for the defense, I don't have much interaction with Deacon or Declan, both of whom have their fair share of drama going on this season. Deacon with an impromptu engagement with the new massage therapist on the medical staff. Declan with a surprise five-year-old son who he is over the moon crazy about. "So your demeanor over the last couple weeks has been an overwhelming need to lie low and avoid your perpetual need to self-sabotage?"

"Yeah."

I nod as we walk off the elevator together. I guess I can't blame him and will support him however he needs. "Let's call our woman, order room service, and chill for the night."

"Sounds good." Jepson slaps my shoulder and squeezes. "I appreciate you, Jaxs."

Using our electronic key card, I'm hit with a wave of love and lust as we enter our room decorated with candles and a congratulations banner.

"Are you alone?" Maryanne calls from the bathroom.

"It's just us," I call back.

She opens the bathroom door wearing silky lingerie. "Congratulations on your big win."

I shake my head. "What? How?"

She approaches us with a big smile on her beautiful face. "London wanted to surprise Deacon and I asked if I could tag along."

Pulling her into my arms, I kiss her softly and brush my thumb over her cheek. "Perfect timing, baby."

Jepson sinks to the edge of the bed and pulls her onto his lap. He wraps his arms around her and buries his face into her neck. "I'm so happy you're here. I fucking love you so much, Maryanne."

She furrows her brow, the concern we've shared over the last couple of weeks written all over her face.

I nod reassuringly, wordlessly telling her it will be okay.

"I love you, too." She curls up in his lap, squeezing him tight with her arms wrapped around him.

"Should we order food?"

She giggles. "You are always hungry."

I lean down and teasingly nibble on her neck and earlobe. "Yes, I am."

"To finish up our conversation in the elevator—" Jepson interjects out of nowhere "—you know what it is, Jaxs? I finally appreciate what I have to lose, and I'm unwilling to lose it. My position on the team, Maryanne, you, and the family we're creating. I'm not going to fuck it up, and if that means I become a mute shut-in, that's what I'll do."

Maryanne cups his face. "What are you talking about?"

"You're concerned about why I've been different the last few weeks? That's why. Nothing is wrong, but I'm protecting what's mine, specifically from myself."

"Babe, that is not sustainable. You are who you are. Loud, energetic, extroverted, a little wild—that's you—and I love you how you are. Sure, maybe we can work on your whole thinking-before-letting-shit-fly problem, but you have twenty-six years to unlearn, and I'm not going to leave because you say one or two dumb things. You love me. I feel it in the way you take care of me, hold me, and talk to me." She reaches out and grabs my hand, guiding me to sit next to Jepson. "I love you both so much. You don't have to worry about losing me."

"Would you marry us?" Jepson asks out of the blue. He glances at me and I can tell by the look on his face he's been thinking about this for some time. "Not today. I'm not proposing or anything, but eventually, can we make a family?"

"Yes, but I'm thirty-three. If we want to have kids, we better make it sooner rather than later." She kisses his jaw and then leans forward, kissing me on the lips. "I would be thrilled to be your wife and the mother of your children. However, I don't want to talk about that tonight. Tonight, I want to eat. I want to make love. And I want to cuddle in my men's arms until the early morning."

"Whatever makes you happy, baby." Jepson and I exchange a look and I know, with her in our life, everything will work out perfectly.

Epilogue
Maryanne - Five Years Later...

"Karina, get off of there and help Karson pick up your toys before bedtime."

We tried. We really did try, but twins with similar names seem inescapable. Besides, their mother's middle name was Karina and I had my heart set on Karson ever since my brother and his wife had their first child. So...

"It's Karson's mess. Let him clean it up." Karina sasses me.

Before I can say anything, Jepson walks into the room with his brow raised in her direction. Karina is a daddy's girl, specifically Jepson's girl, so one disapproving look from him cows her quickly. She climbs off the top of their playhouse to pick up the building blocks that Karson is more playing with than picking up.

Bedtime—it's a process.

Every night.

What is it they say about the terrible twos? They last until college? God, I hope not.

The twins are three years old, a handful, and absolutely perfect in every way. I wasn't expecting to have twins, even though I'm married to them, but I forgot that my father's two older brothers are twins, and my maternal grandmother was also a twin. I guess it was unavoidable and made for a long and tenuous pregnancy.

Jaxson and I officially married at the courthouse with Jepson as a witness in March and then held a private ceremony later that summer after the championship season. It was the summer of weddings. First London and Deacon in February. Then Amelia and Declan in April. Of course, both of their weddings were large, lavish, and highly publicized, not only as big, badass football players, but as Scotts, who are amongst the Spring City elite due to their insane money and political connections.

We had a backyard ceremony with less than twenty attendees—but they were all people who knew and supported our relationship. Of course, it didn't take long for the entire organization to become aware of Jepson and Jaxson's relationship with the "charity chick" and by the next season it was no longer a taboo topic. Any media coverage about any of our relationships was and is quickly squashed by Deidre and her right hand woman, Amelia. The team image as a family focused organization is super important to the Scott's, and they've often reminded the media that each of us choose our family in whatever form that takes, and our football players are champions because of the love and support they receive on and off the field.

"Are we ready for bed?" Jepson puts his hand on my back as he talks to the kids.

"We're not tired." Karina says. She always speaks for both of them as the bossier of the two, and I'm pretty sure that's how Jepson was with Jaxson when they were kids, which is why they bonded like they did.

Karson responds by yawning.

"You're never tired and yet you're always the first one to fall asleep." I hold my hand out to Karson as he stands and puts the last of their building blocks away.

"Bath time." Jaxson walks in, swinging Karson into his arms.

Seeing this, Karina puts her arms up, demanding Jepson do the same—which of course, he does.

Rolling my eyes, I follow my husbands out of the room, letting them take care of baths and the brushing of teeth while I clean the kitchen—only when I get there, it's already spotless. I glance down at our basset hound Chauncey as he digs into his dinner, and then over at Clarence, our big fat orange tabby cat, who sits up on his perch with his own dinner.

I swear, I don't know how women handle life without two husbands. Career, kids, love, house, and home—having two men help me manage it all is about perfect. Three would also work, but I like my two exactly as we have it.

"Story time." Jepson calls from the bedroom, which is my cue to get in there. The twins currently share a room and will until they show a need for independence. It's fascinating to me how similar they are, and yet how individual their personalities are. Makes me all the more curious and enthralled by stories from my husband's childhoods.

Jepson sits on the edge of Karina's bed while Jaxson sits on the edge of Karson's. I take up residence between them in the "mommy chair" between their beds. Every night at seven-thirty—or within minutes of them coming home from practice when it runs late—we read for fifteen minutes or until both kids are knocked out. Usually it only takes ten, but sometimes it takes longer.

Once the kids are asleep, we retire to the living room to cuddle on the couch. We're mid-way through the season and the Rangers are still near the top of the league, winning more games than losing, and always making it to the playoffs. They've won two of the last five championships and dominate their division. Jaxson has been first-string cornerback and ranked in the top three of the league since we've been together. He goes to the Pro Bowl every year.

Jepson is an amazing running back and starts many games. He also went to the Pro Bowl the last two years.

Thanks to London, I understand so much more of the game. Her explanations make so much more sense than my husbands, who explain it like a player versus a fan.

"I wanted to talk to you both about something I've been thinking about." Jepson mutes the TV and changes positions on the couch, wedging himself into the corner. Jaxson pulls me into his lap, so we're both facing him.

"What's up, babe?"

"I'm thinking about making this my last season with the team."

Jaxson tenses. "What? Why?"

"Let's face it, I'm never going to be a top player like you, and the kids are growing up so fast and will be starting school before we know it. I don't want to miss a second more than I have to. Between our jam-packed days and our travel schedules, I wonder if both of us playing is what's best for this family?"

"I thought we'd play together until one of us couldn't play anymore." Jaxson says softly.

"I was thinking maybe I'd get my general contractor license and start a home building company. That way when you were ready to retire from football, our next adventure would be established."

"I thought we were going to do that together."

Sitting quietly, I watch this interchange between my husbands, both of them saddened by the potential change. My heart breaks for them, but I know this is a decision they have to work out between them.

I mean, yes, it affects me and the kids, but this is about more than household dynamics.

"Playing won't be the same if you aren't there." Jaxson shakes his head.

"I know." Jepson nods. "Nothing is set in stone, but I wanted to bring it up. I don't want to do this for another ten years, our bodies broken and battered from nearly twenty years on the field. Eventually, the team might want to trade one of us, and what are we going to do then?"

"Honestly, I figured that would be the trigger to launch this conversation."

"What do you think, Maryanne?" Jepson inches closer and pulls my legs into his lap.

I shrug. "It's hard to say. You both make valid points, but I don't think either of you will be happy not playing together. What if you compromised and set a retirement date?"

"We're completely in sync as a team. It would be crazy to leave now." Jaxson points out.

"Could we give ourselves a five year plan? The kids will be eight, which is about the time they'll be hot and heavy in club sports. I don't want to miss that. Hell, I want to coach if either of them are down with peewee football."

"Good point." Jaxson chuckles and relaxes underneath me. "And who knows, maybe we pull the plug earlier than five years depending upon how the team is doing. Like, maybe the first year we don't make the play-offs will be our sign to hang up our cleats?"

"Or if one of us gets injured." Jepson adds.

"Oh god, please don't say that." I shake my head. That's one thing I'm constantly scared of while watching my men play on the big screen. Everytime one of the sacks or gets sacked by another player, my insides clench until they stand and move across the field without limping. London has shown me clips from when Deacon was temporarily paralyzed, and the images make me want to vomit.

"Don't worry, sweetheart. As long as my mouth and

tongue work, I'll still be able to pleasure you." Jepson slides his hands up my legs and leans forward with a wicked grin on his lips.

"Not funny." I giggle as Jaxson tickles my sides lightly.

Jepson kisses me softly. "Thank you."

"For what?"

"For giving me and Jaxson a safe place to have conversations like this. I can't imagine our lives without you."

"And you don't have to." I cup his face. "Ever."

Jaxson presses his lips to my neck. "Maybe we should bathe our wife and go to bed early?"

"She is dirty." Jepson grins.

"Absolutely filthy." I add, spreading my thighs as his fingers slide between my legs.

"Fuck, I love you." He abruptly stands and offers me his hand, pulling me into his chest and then lifting me in his arms.

Jaxson is on his feet, turning off the lights as Jepson carries me up to our bedroom, murmuring behind me, "We're going to clean you up really good, baby."

"Head to toe and every place in between." Jepson chuckles.

"Especially the places in between." He agrees.

"I love you guys so much." I purr my earthly gratitude as the cat-and-dog-loving, cardigan-wearing, older woman blessed with two husbands who gift her an amazing love-filled life everyday.

Coming Next: Rylie and Sunshine's story Red Zone
Signed paperbacks and bundle discounts are available here.
Subscribe to the Witty, Wicked & Wild Community for early access, bonus epilogues, and more.

Also by Kameron Claire

Want more **Witty** Tongues, **Wicked** Needs, & **Wild** Deeds?

<u>Hollywood Lights (Pre-Order)</u>

** Billionaire Romance **

Show Time (Securing Selyne)

Money Shot

Three Shot

Martini Shot

Long Shot

<u>Veteran K9 Team</u>

** Military Romance **

Mine to Cherish

Mine to Crave

Mine to Possess

Mine to Adore

Mine to Covet

Mine to Worship

Mine to Protect

Mine to Treasure

Hot Nights with the Boss

** Forbidden Office / Age-Gap Romances **

Dating the Boss

Flirting with the Boss

Teasing the Boss

Tempting the Boss

Rangers Football

** Sports Romance **

Play Action Fake

Quarterback Sneak

Personal Foul

Two-Point Conversion

Red Zone

Man to Man Coverage

Short Story Collections and Bundles

Animal Attraction 4-Story Collection

Vegas Nights 4-Story Collection

Last Stand Saloon 4-Story Collection

Instalove Bundle

About the Author

USA Today Bestselling Author Kameron Claire writes stories with witty tongues, wicked needs, and wild deeds. Her books emphasize strong female leads and the protective alpha males who know how to love and support kick-ass, take-charge women. Many of her books contain military veterans, boss babes, gentle but dominant men, and goofy K9 hijinks.

Find her everywhere via linktr.ee/kameronclaire
Signed Paperbacks and discounted eBook bundles are available exclusively on her store
Subscribe to the Witty, Wicked & Wild community and read all her books online for as little as $5 a month.